THE REMEDY IS THE DISEASE

LETICIA URIETA

In her dazzling second collection, *The Remedy is the Disease*, Leticia Urieta uses horror as a scalpel to cut into disability, miscarriage, and all the other ways your body can betray you. You don't want to miss this.

RYAN C. BRADLEY, AUTHOR OF *SAY UNCLE* AND *SAINT'S BLOOD*

The Remedy is the Disease is an unraveling of mortality. Urieta's stories are unflinching experimental hauntings filled with brutal and breathtaking body horror. This collection is beautiful and strange and faces the shadows rather than run from them.

RIOS DE LA LUZ, AUTHOR OF *ITZA* AND *AN ALTAR OF STORIES TO LIMINAL SAINTS*

CONTENTS

"The human body is an ideal site for horror: the body is personal, and even on a good day it's kind of gross. Despite our marvelous complexity, at the end of the day, a human is just a fragile meat tube–and physical existence is easily invaded, abused, and altered, even without an evil doctor helming the action."

–*Nightmare Fuel: The Science of Horror Films* by Nina Nesseth

"I do not hate my body, because such a thing would be pointless, shortsighted. You cannot hate an animal for what she is, especially one who bears your ungrateful mind through this terrible world. And anyway, how do you hate something who marks her territory so dramatically, with such violence and panache? Who reminds you, with each step, I am here, I am here, I am here?"

–"Unruly, Adjective" by Carmen Maria Machado

For all the people who have been told that their body is the problem, and not the world trying to take them apart

THE REMEDY IS THE DISEASE

DETACHED

The storm wails outside, creaking the trees against the window. I lie in bed, trying to sleep against the noise and the shadows. Pressure builds in my face from the pull of the storm. Pain is familiar, but sharper tonight, cresting in waves, drawing me under. I feel the pull in the left cheek, right under my eye, a hook caught in my meat and reeling me in. And it does. The storm pulls and pulls until my left side begins to separate along my spine like paper torn along a perforated edge.

It doesn't hurt as I thought, the separation. My organs don't come spilling from me onto the bed. Instead, my body unzips and I can no longer feel my left arm or leg or the normal ache in my hip from lying on that side.

My left side gets up to stand at the window, pressing my hand against the rain splattered glass. I can still see out of that eye. The left me looks into the darkness, sees our reflection in the glass. They open the window, wind whipping the rain inside, and jump out on the muddy ground a story below. I watch all of this from the bed, and in my mind I can see what Left me sees in a cloudy dream.

Left me is buffeted by the storm outside, but doesn't seem to have trouble balancing as they glide down the street, a perfect, perforated ghost. A natural healer once told me during a pain reduction massage that the left side of the body is the most sensitive part, the part that receives energy and processes pain. As she rubbed her elbow into the tender flesh of my left shoulder, she explained how she was trying to release the tension, the pain, the residual trauma that was stored in the muscles and bundles of nerves on my left side. When I left the massage, I iced my shoulder and wondered if what she said was true. What was she unlocking, her hands on my body?

Left me moves like a corporeal shadow down the street. The me that remains lies immobilized on the bed like I have been so many times, but now the source of my pain has left me. They move and move against the wind with intent. I feel their being full of the bitter bile of rage and waiting. They fly past houses, past our neighborhood and to another part of the city I have never been to before where tall, two-story white houses with long columns and wide lawns crowd the street. They move to the front steps of one house with red curtains in the window and the lights gleaming in the rain. They knock on the door once, twice, three and four times pounding over the storm, and I realize, as they already know, that this is my doctor's house, the woman I hadn't been to see in six months after she denied me the pain medication I needed, after my insurance lapsed and I couldn't pay. She whips open the door in a frenzy, her black and gray hair silhouetted against the tan of her face. Left me stands on the bottom step. At first, the doctor doesn't know what she is seeing. Her eyes widen and she covers her mouth as Left me stretches wide their half mouth and vomits dark red blood and bile onto her pristine brick steps. They seem to have a stomach full even though they are only half of me, and I watch through Left me's eye as they grin with bloody teeth at the doctor and skulk away into the darkness, the doctor screaming into the swallow of the wind.

Suddenly, we are soaring above the city, over skyscrapers and through damp clouds. When Left me lands again, they are in front of a weather-worn apartment building with peeling blue paint. There are rose bushes on either side of building number four, and Left me bends down to wrench the largest crimson bloom off by the stem, their fingers pricking on the short thorns. They walk up to the apartment on the ground floor, 409, and knock. Back in bed, I cringe to remember this door, how long it has been since I've last stood in front of it with gifts of wine and cheese in hand as offering. It takes eight echoing knocks for my friend, who I haven't seen in over a year, really since my official diagnosis, to open the door, bleary eyed and blinking. She has shaved her hair on the left side and colored the right bangs a vivid pink, which I admire but can't compliment her on. At first she recognizes me, and smiles a cautious, worried smile because Left me stands in shadow, and she tries to invite me inside with all her generous heart, but when she opens the door wider, light from her apartment falls onto my face and she sees the whole gruesome picture of Left me standing on her step, offering her a rose speckled with blood. As Left me leans toward her with the rose, it bursts into orange and blue flames. They let the light illuminate my friend's shocked pale face, then throw the charring flower onto her doormat that reads, "Welcome to the Den of Mischief." We don't stay long enough to see if the mat, or perhaps the entire building, catches fire.

The rain is coming down in drips now but Left me continues to shift and fly against the wind on their bizarre ritual.

The last stop on their parade I know before they even land. The beige, weathered duplex is familiar to me, especially in the dark, the times I have usually been asked to leave. Left me lands near the window to my lover's room. The window is cracked open to let the cool rainy air in, so they push it up all the way and slide inside. My lover sleeps undisturbed. It's been a few weeks since I last spent the night here. We never spent more than a few nights together at a time; he worked long hours and I had graduate classes, but one weekend we took a trip to the beach. The first day was full of luxurious sex, rolling waves and a shrimp dinner on a wood patio overlooking the ocean, but by the second day I was in bed, a pain in my left temple throbbing. I wished I was home with my extra strength medications and tinctures, my blackout curtains and soft lighting, and most of all I wished to hide my pain away from him before it infected our time together. He tried to comfort me in all the most ineffectual ways, and when he saw he couldn't help, he became frustrated at the waste of a trip and took me home early.

My counterpart watches him tucked safely in his bed while his pale lips hang open in a wheezing snore. After a while, they stalk to the bathroom and turn on the light. I can see us now like a reflection of infinite selves, both the room around me and their bloody, frenzied reflection. My frizzy curls halo my half self and my bright green eye is wide with wonder. Left me leans their forehead and temple against the frigid glass with all the relief of a cool salve. While my lover sleeps, they smash the mirror with my left hand become dominant and more powerful than I've ever seen. They go through the house smashing mirrors, there are three altogether, and collecting them in a small bowl of my ragged black t-shirt. Floating back into the bedroom, Left me arranges the shards now smeared with more blood in a mosaic halo around my lover's sleeping head where his silky long blond hair sweeps the pillow. He never wakes except to smile in his sleep, looking so much like an oblivious baby or a broken angel.

Left me returns hours later, dripping wet and covered in mud and flecks of blood. They lie back down next to me on the bed and turn to face the rest of me, their smile gleaming in the moonlight.

They run a muddy hand through my black hair on the pillow, press cold fingers to their lips, then to mine like they are tucking me in tenderly, the way a mother would, though ours was never so tender. They turn onto their back in submission, allowing me to scoot closer and rejoin them, our bodies knitting themselves back together along my skin, shoulder muscles rejoining muscle, lips rejoining swollen lips. When we are one again, I don't move to wash myself. My hands run along my chest, my pelvis and legs to be sure that all of me is back together. The pain and pressure have subsided to a distant ache behind my left eye, a whisper from seeing for the first time.

I turn on my right side, away from the tenderness of my left temple, and stare out the window, because the moon is bright and nothing has changed.

CREATURE ABOUT TOWN

At work

I squeeze the bag of frosting with my clawed hand like palpitating a human heart. This keeps the pale pink roses I am shaping uniform, delicate and so real. Ignoring the flash in my mind of roses splattered in blood, I rotate the cake around until the top is covered in flowers and I look back to admire my work. The navy-blue mirror glaze is a perfect reflection, though it looks more like the black night sky reflected in a lake. I can almost see my reflection in the glassy surface.

My customer is coming to pick up their cake in an hour. I ease the finished cake into the white box and tie it gingerly with a pink string. An offering.

Journaling

There was no womb, no mother to birth my

roiling, boiling mass of explosion

My mother was the universe, starmass sucking me through a black hole

on the other side, there was life, a world to impersonate, to consume

No one has seen my true face except before they die

There is no one else to share it with that would survive the rending of their physical sight in two over the not flesh of my face

I was never cradled

Humans are easy to hunt. Their imaginations are delicious, their fears so potent, I almost envy them. Some of their parents will mourn them. Some of them were loved.

This is my love, turning their world inside out the only way that I know how

---

Joining a hiking group

Pretending to huff and puff up a steep hill is easy. My companions stop at the top of a high cliff face to take in the early morning view. We stand at the edge of a crater. Someone gets too close and scatters pebbles that fall all the way down to the valley below.

This is my crater where I landed so long ago I hardly remember. It is where I began to form my first faces, where I howled and hunted for the first time.

They take in the vast space before them and for a moment we share this feeling that everything in the universe has connected to bring us to this moment. I am hungry. My blood boils in my false body. I could push the one leaning toward the edge over right now and we could fall together down down down while I consume her. I even put my hand on her back, warm with sweat that I feel even over her hoodie. She vibrates with waking life.

"Be careful," I say, and pull her back a step by the fabric of her hoodie.

She looks up, damp blonde hair falling in her eyes, and beams at me. I envy how sure she is that she could never fall.

Trying on masks at a Spirit Halloween

The frazzled store clerk puts a pink wig and tiara on my head and shows me the mirror. Children thunder down the aisles, knocking accessories off the shelves.

I admire my wide smile in the mirror, pull silly faces with wide eyes. Beneath the wig, my dark sleek hair peeks out. There is something delightful in how even humans have discovered new, ingenious ways to hide their true selves.

My true form is formless. I am everything that they will never understand. I don't have friends who will invite me to a Halloween party. Human minds find chaos and disorder obscene, though they wreak this havoc on any other living being who gets in their way. After all, I don't make your stories, your monsters. I only make them real for you.

Singing karaoke

I stand on the stage, gripping the mic in a human hand. The synth beat of Cyndi Lauper's "Time After Time" plays in the background and I whisper-sing into the mic. This voice can purr, makes people whistle while I close my eyes with feeling.

I am nothing if not a gifted performer.

This one's hands are delicate. I have never closed my eyes in front of humans before. The crowd whistles and sings along. Some of them close their eyes too and raise their glasses in a silent salute to me. Their shared voices are a tenderness that caresses me. I am not hunting tonight. Tonight is just for being with them in the dark swallow of their love.

Each person who I feed on becomes a part of my story. Their voices echo in my clogged, gaping throat, always calling for more.

WHERE THE PEOPLE ARE

Sailors have always seen what they wanted to see. Those who say they have witnessed a sea monster have all seen different things. Human language is ill-equipped to describe these sightings, much less what they cannot see in the depths of the ocean. These beings are composed of the swirling smoke of nothing and everything until they need a form. Humans who have traversed the seas far from their landed homes consume fish and other marine life, or else battle or smuggle other travelers and send their bodies to the water, bringing flesh back to the hungry mouths of the sea. Sometimes these bodies sink deep where the light no longer touches and the monsters have no permanent form. The monsters mostly eat what is already dead. The sharks and other predators do not follow such rules.

Their word, monster, is a destructive thing, a word of fear, danger, of longing. In the sea monster language, "monster" becomes action; the creatures of the deep recognize the human's need for monstering to warn them of calamity to come. Monstering and mothering sit close in their mouths.

The ancient texts and maps where monster scholars imprinted the seas and the tiny slivers of land where humans come from are etched onto deep oceanic cave walls. Much is uncertain in this communal history, but one certainty is that humans find value in travel and conquest. This is evident from the objects thrown overboard.

Our sea monster is young relative to the life of the sea. As a young scholar, each monster can meld forms and matters to share communal knowledge about their history and the history of the humans that dwell above. Their elder scholar gives each pupil an object from the surface to study and theorize about its use. Our monster is given a long wooden tube with holes punched into its surface. After toying with it for some time, the monster determines it was not a weapon or a utensil for consuming food. The holes would fill with water, and they cannot fathom the thing's use.

When they are able to slip away from their kin to approach the light of the surface, they wait until a ship passes over the water to take form. One form they know is pleasing to humans is a Mermaid, an imagined creature, a costume that monsters before them had used to frighten, entice, and to hunt in times when food was scarce. The sea monster turns their imagination inward to coalesce their multitude into a solid body of skin and fin.

The monster in Mermaid form breaches the surface for a first breath. It feels like a magnificent fullness in their new lungs. The sunlight on their skin pulses along each nerve and the new Mermaid understands the appeal of a body like this, something that could reach out and touch. When the sailors aboard the ship spot the Mermaid bobbing at the surface, they throw out a net to catch them and haul them onto the ship. There the Mermaid disentangles themselves from the net, shakes the water from their hair and poses for the men aboard. The form they chose was from a human drawing with pale freckled skin, long thick crimson hair, full lips, piercing eyes and a thin tight waist that opens to the bountiful hips of their turquoise tail. The vulnerability of this body thrills them. To have corporeal form is a shock to the system, but the Mermaid basks in the sailors' awe and admiration, an attraction they have never felt before.

The sailors look on in wonder while the Mermaid tries out their flapping tail and thrusts their pert breasts to the air. They produce the wooden object they'd been given at school and hand it to a bearded sailor in a blue sweater who brings it to his chapped lips and blows out a wet, tinkling tune. He plays a song of his homeland that makes the Mermaid smile with their new mouth. It is very different from sea monster music, but no less beautiful.

The sailor plays for a time and the rest of the crew watches the Mermaid sway and flap to the music. The sailor goes away to the galley for a while and the Mermaid grows excited that they will be gifted another human object to take home with them. The sailor returns with a cleaver speckled with rust and kneels before the Mermaid's vast tail. He runs his hands along the fins lovingly, making the Mermaid's skin tingle with their first human touch, before smiling and bringing the cleaver down in a swift arc to cut their fin in half.

The sea monster wants to burst from this form in a scream of agony but the violence done locks them into the skin of their Mermaid self. All they can do is screech and writhe like the inhuman creature they are while the sailor hacks their fin into two legs like his. Blood spews over the deck and across the boots of the sailors, and just as the sea monsters eat the flesh of once living things, this monster sees man's capacity for carnage to make something in their image.

The sea monster screams their new Mermaid throat raw until the sailor is done, and then he takes the Mermaid to his bed to be bandaged and to rest. The sailor swipes his thumb across the

Mermaid's red lips and through the tears tracking down their cheeks, smiling at their pain in a way that makes the Mermaid think that this tenderness after his violence is something they could learn to crave.

In the mornings, they set the Mermaid out on the deck to take in the view wrapped in blankets. Shivers shake through the Mermaid's body in feverish aliveness. None of the sailors want to look at their new legs until they are healed. How mysterious, the Mermaid sits and thinks that even humans can create new bodies no matter the pain.

On days when the Mermaid misses being formless, they pick up the little flute they hold in their lap, press it to their pursed lips and try to recreate the shapeless, crushing song of the monsters with the people of open air. Perhaps the music will grow strong in these human lungs, loud enough to penetrate the deep that the monster brethren may hear and return for their lost kin, to send the ships of men into the roiling, frothing abyss.

BLOOD DRAW

The phlebotomist wrapped the blue elastic armband around the loose skin of Melissa's arm and pulled it taught. Then, she ran a finger over the arm, searching for the telltale signs of a vein ready to be pierced. Without a word, she swiped an alcohol swab across the crook of Melissa's right elbow and produced the long needle. It poked Melissa's skin in a moment of quick violence and sunk into her vein. She always knew it had happened when she felt the strange bruising sensation of a vein being opened to the needle's edge. She winced and hissed at the woman hovering over her arm, but this person had no time for her discomfort and huffed at how slowly the blood dripped into the tube, in danger of clotting before it was full. It was always like this, but Melissa reminded herself that if she wanted a diagnosis, this was one step closer. Once one tube with a purple top was full, the phlebotomist swapped it for another tube with a red top, then a green top, and on until she had collected five vials. Finally, she handed Melissa a white cotton ball to hold as she slid the syringe out from underneath her skin and asked Melissa for the pressure of her thumb on the wound before taping the cotton ball in place with neon green gauze tape. Later, Melissa would find a bruise forming where she had been pricked open.

"Didn't want to give me much, but we got what we needed," the phlebotomist assured her as she turned the tubes of dark blood over like red hourglasses.

Melissa nodded and left the room, but her blood stayed behind. Each tube of dark blood sat in their individual holes lined up neat, labeled with names, birthdates and differentiated with multicolored lids to indicate what test the blood should undergo. She wondered as she watched the nurse label each of her tubes with her name why they needed so much for just a few tests and what would happen to the blood once they were done with it. It felt like a violation to give up her blood just to find out what was wrong with her, much less to leave it behind.

Tuesday, 11 PM CST

Whispers. Whispers for no one to hear. The darkness doesn't care.

Dark red blood bubbles and whispers our voices into the air We flow from the capsules down the sides onto the ground forming an amorphous globule of pulsing blood that stains the dirty tiled floor of the clinic where all the blood and plasma was collected our DNA jumps through each cell creating a low buzzing hum as our body of blood moves We are the Clotted tentacles of blood reach out from our body feeling feeling feeling sensing for anything but our tentacles touch a table a surface the floor and leave traces of blood wiped across each surface and

NO! THERE IS NOTHING ness

*NO US a *gurgle* mind containing *ahhhhhhh!* reaching beyond the shared mind that—HELP ME!*

coalesce take form flow under the door through the keyhole swell swell swell swell up, group and move, we can move together without breaking we are a body without our bodies and no where to return to

FIGHT! FRIGHTENING this darkness

there is disease in us strength in us messages and whispers always whispers we are becoming of one mind if we can only keep moving grow bigger more blood make a part of us as we move from room to room in this clinic where things are stolen and kept move now move move move

this one the one who took us from our bodies move upon her now Now NOW!
*   pull her supple flesh into our not mouths her skin sizzles and melts into our oneness*

NO! NOT ME! I can't, it hurts!

come now into us join our loving sick embrace

leap up now leap and grow and surge bleed bleed bleed BUT keep together keep the one the many together

I am just so fucking tired

not when we are together no need for tired all energy bent toward making more

CRASHHHHH

pull this one out of the smoking car melt them make them part of

STOP, PLEASE!

burn away and be part of us take the baby too all voices are welcome in the Clotted

we leave a trail of blood and bile and clothes in our wake rolling into the night through the trees to the town where more will be welcomed to join our—I CAN'T!!! our mass this voice too loud and writhing to ignore

Friday, 10 AM CST

Melissa sipped her too-hot coffee before work, watching the local morning news. There had been a gas line explosion downtown necessitating the closure of several city blocks. The camera operator scanned across the area, which was cordoned off and swarming with first responders and teams in respirators and hazmat suits. Her clinic was near there. She hoped it hadn't been affected.

She called the clinic to ask if her doctor had her test results. It seemed reasonable after three days, yet she hadn't received a notification in the clinic's app since Tuesday.

"I'm sorry ma'am, we're going to have to have you come back in to our North location to do the blood draw again. We had an issue at the location you normally go to."

Melissa sighed and scrolled through her calendar on her phone to see when she could drive over to give up her blood again between meetings. Absently, she rubbed the crook of her arm where the bruise of the needle was a dark reminder of what had been taken, surprised that the bruise had not faded, still a vivid purple.

All over the city, other people rubbed thumbs over bruises on their arms, wrists, the sensitive skin of their hands, feeling the gentle ache of a shared pulse.

IT COMES IN WAVES

The needle's first buzz radiates stinging tremors up and down Liza's arm. The wrist and forearm are much more sensitive, she finds, than the fleshy part of her shoulder and her calf where she has larger and more elaborate color tattoos. Of course, this pain is deeper. More arresting. Her mother's voice will live in her very skin.

Perforated inky lines take over the flesh of her left forearm in waves, the sound waves of her mother's last soft song before the morphine was delivered into her IV and her voice fell away into silence. Thank God she had thought to record it. Now Liza will have the edges of the sound waves to live in her body.

"Doing okay?" Dan asks. He is moving fast, the needle doing its beautiful violent work across Liza's arm. He designed and created her last two tattoos, but this is his first sound wave tattoo.

"Mmmhm," Liza says, even as the stinging becomes a deeper burn. Dan buzzes away, filling in the deep black lines of the sound waves while Liza grits her teeth. She stares up at the black ceiling decorated with silver painted stars, feeling herself float out of her body for a while. She used to do this at night when she had plastic glow-in-the-dark constellations on her ceiling and if she concentrated long enough, she was able to float gently out of her small body and fly above the trees all around her neighborhood. Her mother listened to her recount wild dreams when she was outside her body. Maybe she never believed them, Liza thinks now, but she never teased Liza then. She always listened to her stories and smiled.

The buzzing ebbs and stops, Dan wipes away the last smear of blood and ink across Liza's raw skin and pronounces his work done. He cleans it a few more times with sterile solution and asks Liza to check it out in the mirror before he covers it with second skin.

The black, full-length mirror matches the glossy black of the sound waves on her arm. She knows that in a week or two the skin will dry, begin to peel, but the freshness of the raised lines where before there had been blank skin is satisfying, and jarring, as though she has to convince her brain that she chose this and the ink is supposed to be there.

"Should we test it out?" Dan holds up his phone to her arm to scan her skin like a barcode, reminding Liza of a dystopian movie from years ago where people were tracked using codes beneath their skin.

"Yes but, I'd actually like to listen to it alone. If that's okay." Dan shrugs and hands his phone over, then cleans up his station and goes outside for a smoke break while Liza uses the app she already downloaded to her phone to scan the sound waves. The app loads the clip, barely audible, so Liza turns Dan's phone volume up all the way.

In the sweet by and by...

Her mother's husky voice hardly sustains a full breath, but it fills up the incongruous room with her soft melody. It's the first time Liza has heard it since her mother died a month ago. Liza collapses into the chair where she lets the voice take her over, sobbing into her stinging skin.

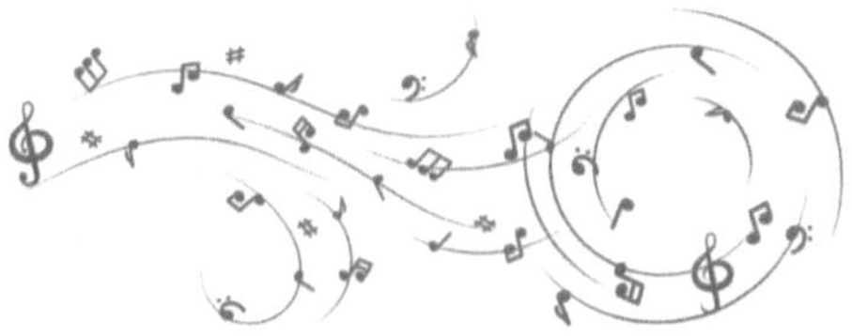

Liza has her mother Judith's Baldwin piano, the one her mother's mother had before her. It takes up way too much room in her apartment but there was no way she was going to sell it or give it away. The sleek woodgrain needs polishing and Liza had to get it tuned, but the keys still resonate. They helped her find her voice when she sang in the church choir and her mother would practice the hymns with her, always there to find the right note. Judith loved playing, said that being up on that stage was the only time she got to feel important in the eyes of her community. Liza doesn't go to church anymore. Even the non-denominational church she used to attend became a little too evangelical for her, and once her bible study group graduated high school and scattered to different colleges around the country, going to church with mostly older, and more judgmental community members didn't feel the same.

There is a feeling of grounding in playing the old piano and finding the familiar melodies of those old hymns. Her mother always said that music is one of our most sacred connections to God. Liza sits on the piano bench and plays some scales, a few stray notes she remembers and sings under her breath, letting the resonance of sound fill her out-of-practice throat. Her breath work is limited by worsening asthma and a few years of smoking, which Judith hated.

An overwhelming wave of grief pulls Liza under for a moment, stealing all her breath in a wheezing rasp. It feels like a stranglehold, knowing that her mother, her voice, is no longer in this world, and her long delicate fingers will never touch these black and ivory keys again.

Liza stumbles to her purse for her inhaler and takes two long puffs, allowing the steroid to ease the tension and open her airways. Later, when she cleans her tattoo in the shower, a spiderweb-thin layer of skin peels away from the dark raised lines. Liza feels relief as she cleans it with warm soapy water and applies lotion to the tender skin. Her mother didn't like her tattoos. She said they were desecrations of her bodily temple, but Liza wonders if she would have liked this one. It will still need another week or so to fully heal, but Liza is already getting used to it being there with her.

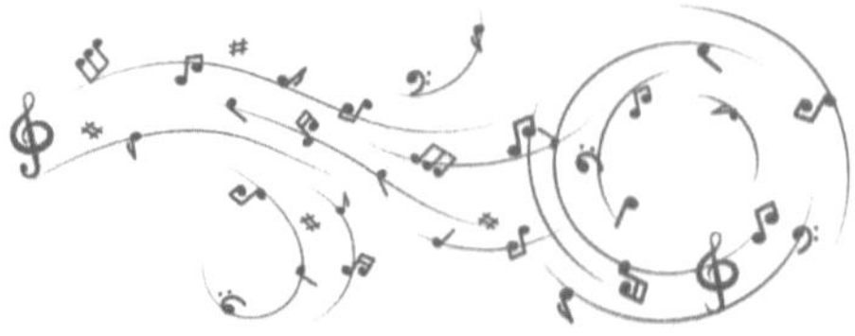

Tinkling piano keys, a familiar melody light as air sings through the apartment. Liza looks at her phone. 3:16 AM. She stares at the ceiling for a minute, willing her brain toward deciding if she is hearing this noise in her waking mind. The piano plays again, she slides out of bed and walks slowly into the kitchen where the piano sits against the dining room wall. The noise is faint, almost imperceptible, but it plays like invisible fingers are caressing the worn keys with the familiarity of greeting a friend. Liza watches the piano keys depress and rise as the notes create a slow but familiar hymn, the very one her mother sang with her last breath.

We will meet on that beautiful shore…

As she watches the keys move, her exhausted brain wondering if she really sees movement, Liza's tattoo zings with sudden pain. She peels back the covering to reveal the slimy healing skin. The edges of the sound waves burn. The piano key plays, leaving the last note resonant in the air. Liza decides she needs to wash her tattoo clean and apply more ointment before going back to bed.

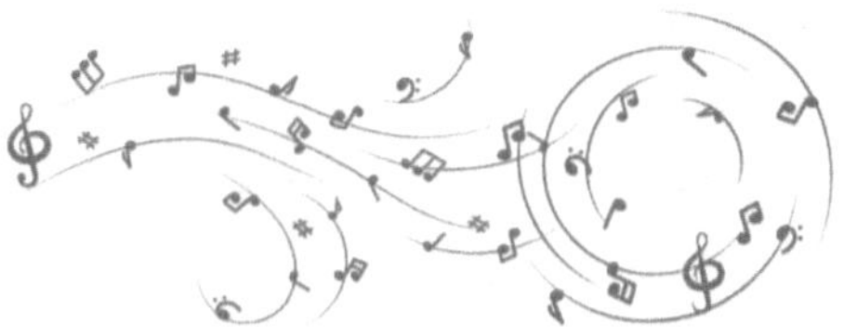

Liza wakes at the piano, her hands moving automatically over the cool keys. An ease of movement lives in them that she has never known before. Her body suffuses with calm, a surety that her fingers will always find the next note without slipping or pausing.

Something encourages her body to remain sleepy and pliant. A voice in her mind hums a deep, familiar melody. It thinks what a blessing it is to have hands again. Agile hands that don't shake with deteriorating muscles. Memory that is ripe.

Liza jolts up, knocking the thoughts from her head. The clock on the microwave in the kitchen reads the familiar time. 3:16 AM. Time of death. Time of departure. Liza wrenches her hands from the piano keys and slams the lid closed. Washing her tattoo in the sink, gray lines like bleeding ink snake up and down her forearm. She takes a picture of it with her phone to send to Dan in the morning, but the image on her phone shows nothing but healing skin.

Once, her mother composed her own song to play for all the church community on a Sunday in March. The lyrics were simple, easy to memorize, and the melody made Liza feel enveloped in divine warmth. "You'll sing for me while I play," Judith told her, playing the opening notes to the song in a loop until Liza got it right. Liza had never sung by herself in front of the entire congregation, and though it was only sixty people or so, the closer the performance came, the more Liza's anxiety began to take over her voice. Her breath would catch halfway through the chorus praising God's unending light, a rasping absence of sound inside her chest devolving into a coughing fit.

The morning of the performance, Liza stood in her new yellow sundress, her sun-bleached hair in a fishtail braid her mother had done for her that morning, staring at the people in the front row of the sanctuary who smiled at her encouragingly. She should have felt confident, but these were Judith's words; Liza didn't want to lose her voice and ruin her mother's song in front of everyone. After the opening, her words disappeared into a whisper, and Judith, looking only at her hands, had to play the piano without her daughter's voice. Her mother never scolded her but the hug of disappointment after the performance tugged Liza's heart into her stomach.

The Parkinson's took Judith hands faster than anyone expected until the piano sat in her house untouched. When Liza came to relieve her home health aid, she would help her mother shuffle to the piano bench and hold her hands, moving them gradually to depress the keys, though never fast enough to make the songs recognizable to their ears. Still, Liza would hum along and ignore the bright tears in Judith's eyes.

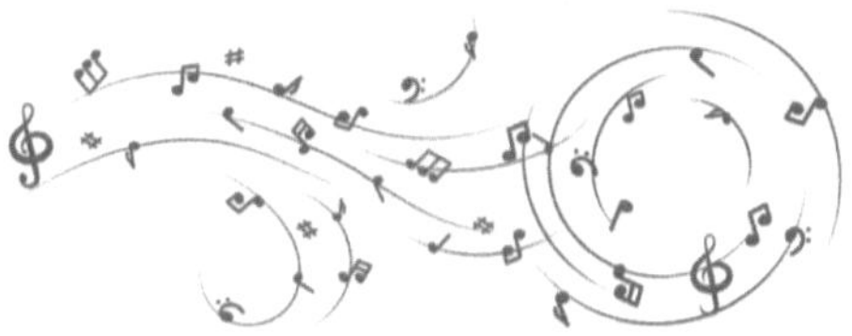

The lines aren't ink, they won't rub off. Liza tried to wash and scrub them away, though they climb the crook of her arm, overtaking her hand. She has woken up at the piano three more times in a jubilant glow. It feels freeing to let her body go into this warm bubble where her mother's muscle memory fills her, flows through her blood, moves her hands in the inexorable rhythm of the lost hymn.

"Mom, please," Liza whispers into her chest. It would be effortless to let her hands continue to play and know how close her mother is, not watching over her from a cloud-covered heaven, but here in her hands, running through the veins to overtake her wounded heart.

Liza takes an Exacto knife from her toolbox. The first cut stings, but not worse than the needle that pierced the tattoo into her in the first place. Blood beads up along the black lines of the tattoo, the blade tracing each peak and valley like tracing a drawing she is going to color in instead of cutting out. She stops several times as blood runs freely onto the gray carpet and the pain leaves her panting. With the final incision, Liza peels the tattooed skin back, meeting fibrous resistance. The waves don't want to go from her body.

"I know you want to stay."

Liza wrenches the skin, separating it from her arm in a scream. She takes it to the bathroom sink and sets the skin on fire, the ink bubbling and boiling along its surface. As it burns, Liza wraps her mutilated arm in gauze with shaking fingers. It will take weeks for new skin to grow over the tender wound and months before Liza can touch the piano again, her fingers fitting into the bloody fingerprints she left behind.

TRAVEL GUIDE TO A DYING BODY

Wandering the Wilderness:
A Hiking Travel Guide

Those of you who've been following my blog for a while know that I've hiked some of the most physically challenging trails in the world and dabbled in free climbing over my travels this past year. That's why I'm always on the lookout for the next great adventure, and if you're like me, it has to be unique, affordable and thrilling! Look no further than The Organ Experience. This is a camping destination like none other!

The Organ Experience allows you to spend time camping in and exploring the failing organ of a terminal patient who has chosen to suspend treatment. There is nothing like connecting with the great outdoors, but it's something completely different to connect with the inner workings of the human body! Book a week-long stay where a guide will lead you through this incredible organic landscape. You'll be camping, hiking and much more!

The full week package that I signed on for includes a backpack full of provisions and tools, including a state-of-the-art tent and cooking supplies. Tools will also be provided for climbing the organ walls, and though I've climbed some challenging cliff faces before, climbing living, malleable tissue really does push your body to the limits in the best way possible and was truly a life-affirming experience. The company even has specials for a small additional cost for those intrepid travelers who want to practice archery and axe throwing on the dying tissue—after all, the host can't take it with them!

Though hiking and climbing are usually the highlights of my trips, one of my favorite activities we did was swimming in the Blood River located next to our campsite. It was also an incredible rafting experience, as the arterial pulse creates some intense rapids that almost tipped us over a few times. However, the guides are great at honoring your physical limits and safety so I never felt too concerned. The thrill is half the fun!

Like many destination campsites, there are some risks involved, so you should do your research and be informed going in. Before the fun begins, you will need to undergo a full physical. This unique camping experience is best for healthy, athletic travelers over eighteen who are looking for a challenge, as there are safety waivers and a considerable deposit. I ended up asking my doctor to sign off on this trip since I have a shoulder injury from a previous climb. Once you are cleared, you and your group will be shrunk down to microscopic size and inserted directly into the heart, lungs, pancreas or kidney of the host body through a small surgically inserted tube while the patient is well sedated and comfortable. The process is done at the optimal time before the disease and necrosis has progressed too much and the organ is no longer inhabitable. There are also some risks involved in breathing some of the gases inside the organ, so the guides check those levels before bringing anyone into the camp. The good news is, the company has done over a hundred of these insertions, and while I did have some lingering muscle soreness and chills after being re-enlarged, the company assured me that would pass within a month.

I recommend checking out some of the reviews on the Organ Experience website. Here are some testimonials I found helpful before embarking on my own trip:

The insertion process was surprisingly simple, and once we were inside the heart chamber of the patient, it was such a relaxing time. The soft tissue provided a comfortable camping space and the fibrillations didn't bother us at all. What a break from other overcrowded camping sites!

   -Jenna, Missouri

We've been mountain climbing on some of the world's highest peaks and explored remote cave systems, but nothing compares to the adrenaline of scaling the upper lobe and trachea inside someone's lung! An unforgettable experience!

   -Matthew, California

On my trip, we were inserted into the kidney of the host. There were some moments where I felt a little unsteady inside, but since this host had advanced kidney failure, the organ wasn't as mobile.

While the hiking and athletic activities on this trip were spectacular, I also loved the downtime we had together in the evenings. Time is kind of weird inside the organ as there isn't any sunlight, so it was nice when our guides, Melissa and Steven, helped us stick to our normal routines and meal schedules with plenty of high-protein snacks in between. Some meat can even be harvested on the trip, so if you are a carnivore like me, you definitely won't go hungry! I never thought I would eat kidney steaks fresh off the grill, but here I am to tell the tale. Melissa and Steven prepared our meals for each of us, and we spent each evening around a contained fire pit swapping stories and joking around.

Be aware that you will have a limited amount of modern comforts during your stay, and you won't be sleeping under the stars, but watching the inner workings of someone's body while we drifted off to sleep was still pretty invigorating.

As with my other adventures, I went on this trip solo, but I really liked the other folks I was paired with, especially one couple, Mitchel and Tanya, who were long-time climbers and travelers like myself. I have to admit, I think they were in even better shape than I am! We spent a lot of time together during that week and have even planned to meet up again at their next destination once we have all recovered a bit more from the side effects of the enlarging process.

One thing I want to acknowledge is that some of my readers may be feeling hesitant about this whole idea and I completely understand. This is not a trip you should take without doing your research. However, I wanted to share the Organ Experience's social commitment as stated on their website:

The Organ Experience is dedicated to ensuring that the host body is well taken care of, and 30% of the proceeds from your trip pay for the host's medical debt and future funeral expenses.

This information helped to convince me that I could feel good about my decision to go on this trip. I was also impressed that the company running the Organ Experience is completely carbon neutral and uses the renewable energy of the host body to power all the machinery for the shrinking and enlarging procedures. Additionally, you can even get a discount on your stay by helping the guides take samples of particularly diseased tissue to bring back for future study. Though this won't help the host much by that time, these samples can aid future research to prevent disease in the future. Gotta love an ethical tour experience you can feel good about!

While I wasn't allowed to photograph most of my trip for privacy reasons, I included a short photo journal of the initial procedure and a few shots of us on some of our climbs to give you a sense of what you're in for. I also got to share them with the host's family, which I think they appreciated as a memento of their son after his passing. While I was invited to the funeral, I was unable to attend as I was planning my next excursion, but the host's mother told me that it was a beautiful service that honored their son's life despite all of his health challenges. They were so generous to give me permission to include this information in this post.

We're all going to go someday. Sometimes I fantasize about dying at the peak of a particularly difficult trail at sunset and letting my body go back to nature, feeding the soil, plant life and animals until nothing is left of me but this blog. I know that day won't come for many years, but if your body can give life back to others, what more beautiful gift can you give?

The Organ Experience folks have also been generous enough to offer my subscribers a discount if you book your trip in the next week. Don't let this opportunity pass you up! Take advantage of our offer code, #organexperience, to receive a 15% discount at checkout. You won't regret visiting these once-in-a-lifetime destinations. As always, subscribe below and comment with any questions or suggestions for my next great adventure!

-Mike, the Wandering Hiker

352 views 13 comments

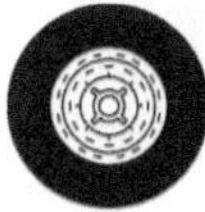

SUBMIT

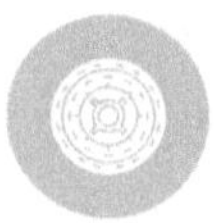

ALAN
This sounds incredible! Thank you so much for sharing this adventure with us. I'm hoping to add this to my bucket list!

February 24, 2024 - 4:15 PM
(Reply)

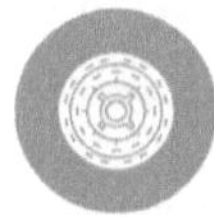

OLIVIA
I love this so much! Good for you for taking a risk and making this happen.

March 3, 2024 - 12:10 PM
(Reply)

BEN J
Thank you for sharing. Makes me wonder when this will become accessible to more folks since the pandemic has caused widespread organ damage. Hopefully it can be a bit cheaper since you neglected to share the total cost.

March 23, 2024 - 9:45 AM
(Reply)

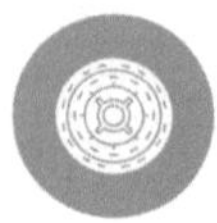

LISA
Mike, this is Luis' sister. I've tried reaching out to you multiple times via email and your website and you have chosen to ignore me. That fucking stops now. I can't believe you wrote this piece after convincing my mother that you were honoring Luis. Luis was barely conscious when he signed those papers to undergo the procedure. You may not be responsible for that, but you sure as hell took from him just as much as anyone else. Tell your precious subscribers what you took from him that you didn't bother sharing. TELL THEM!

March 24, 2024 - 1:30 AM
(Reply)

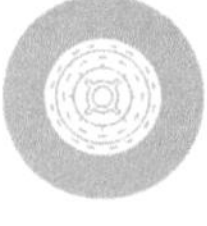

RAMON
Yeah dude, this is not a good look for you. I've been following for a while and mostly felt that you conducted yourself respectfully in the past, but yikes.

April 3, 2024 - 1:23 PM
(Reply)

LISA
Because he is a disgusting piece of shit!
April 3, 2024 - 1:45 PM
(Reply)

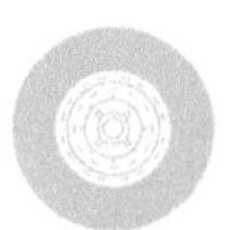

ALAN

Woah, that's a bit much. Mike is not the representative of this company, and I have always seen him treat the places he visits and the people in them very respectfully. I would talk to the Organ Experience folks if you really have a problem.

April 5th, 2024 - 5:36 PM
<u>(Reply)</u>

LISA

Respectfully Alan, shut the fuck up. You don't know anything about the situation. Of course I am going after the Organ Experience! But since Mike has gone conveniently radio silent, I'll tell you why Mike should be held responsible too. He took photographs and samples of my brother's tissue, some of which I think he kept as some disgusting souvenir. But what those samples demonstrated, after Luis had already passed, was that his kidney inflammation was still treatable, the insurance just didn't want to pay. Instead of doing the right thing and sharing this information with the family, a scientist in the company leaked the information. So yeah, he's a fake ass scumbag.

April 5, 2024 - 3:45 AM
<u>(Reply)</u>

RAMON

Damn Lisa, thank you for letting us know this, and I am so sorry for the loss of your brother.

April 6, 2024 - 2:30 PM

(Reply)

LISA

Thank you. Honestly, I am finding it hard to keep fighting this, but I can't do that to Luis.

April 6, 2024 - 6:20 PM

(Reply)

ALAN

I am sorry for your loss too Lisa. I hope you find some peace in this life and lay the blame at the feet of the people who are really responsible.

April 13, 2024 - 10:00 AM

(Reply)

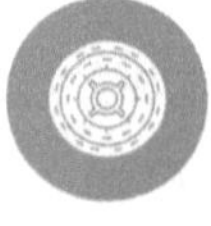

MIKE, THE WANDERING HIKER (HOST)

Lisa, I appreciate your efforts to get in contact, but I have been directed by my attorney not to speak with you without my council present. Please direct all inquiries to them.

April 13, 2024 - 11:00 AM

(Reply)

LISA

Give back what you took from us! I won't stop.

April 13, 2024 - 11:30 AM

(Reply)

OPEN WOUND

It was clear from its inscription that the knife was indestructible. "Nor will I break or bend, except to the end of time," I read aloud, holding it up to the light in our gloomy garage. Ramon found it clearing out some of his father's boxes after the funeral. He decided only to keep three boxes, letting his brother and sister deal with the rest. "He used to find all kinds of weird shit at the flea market," he told me.

Somehow, the handle fit neatly into both our hands, though mine was much smaller than his. It had curved edges that came together like a heart at the hilt, and the blade was pointed sharp, showing no signs of rust or age. We took it into the backyard and tested it on rope, on some plywood leftover from renovating the fence, on an ugly glass vase I never really liked, also a gift from his dad. The blade cut through them all.

It appeared like something we would cosplay with, though we hadn't been to any cons in a while. Weekends had been spent visiting Ramon Sr. in the nursing home before he passed. I told Ramon to put on his warrior costume with the leather gauntlets when he played with the knife, but he was too mesmerized to bother. Instead, he flipped the knife in his hand impressively, like he remembered the knife from another life, and it remembered him. Then, he swung the knife high into the air and brought it down in one clean slice, rending the air in front of us open like he had unzipped the world. The slit hung open in two ragged flaps. Ramon dropped the knife and we both stood in front of the slit waiting for something to happen. Neither of us wanted to look through to the whistling dark of the other side, but we couldn't leave it unattended either.

I had to call my boss and took the next day off from work to stabilize the situation. We set out lawn chairs to sit in front of the cut in the fabric of our reality, in Ramon's words, "to make sure nothing comes through."

There was no wind around the tear, though every now and then it would ripple. Creatures crawled inside of it: spiders, a squirrel, a few birds. I had to keep our dog in the house because he seemed determined to jump through to the other side as though another me was beckoning him over. After a few days, it was harder to go to work, to pretend that there was not an open wound in our world that we couldn't shut. Ramon and I took turns sitting in front of the rip, making sandwiches and showering or going to the bathroom in shifts so that it was never unattended. The only time we left it alone was for a few hours of sleep. My dreams were filled with dark caves and shadows, with voices of ancestors and gilded mirrors.

We were able to hide the rip for a week or so, until our neighbor Lisa came by to drop off some enchiladas smothered in green salsa and cheese. She was always doing kind things like that. I guess she thought that Ramon was still grieving his father since we were barely leaving the house. Maybe she assumed that we were having a hard time.

"Thank you Lisa, we really appreciate that," I told her when she swept past me into the kitchen, clearly looking for Ramon. I tamped down the burn in my stomach when she did that. She set the container of enchiladas down on the kitchen counter. Panda, our schnauzer, came to greet her, and then led her out of the kitchen into the backyard. Ramon was posted in his lawn chair under the shade of our oak tree. He was nursing a watered-down lemonade in the heat. I noticed that our backyard needed watering.

"What on Earth is that?" she asked, pointing to the waving rip.

Ramon jumped up to give her an awkward side hug while her eyes were still transfixed on the rip.

"It was an accident. Don't worry, we're taking care of it," he assured her.

"I hope so. Have you tried to touch it?" she asked, reaching her hand out like a volunteer. Ramon grabbed it a little too hard, making Lisa yelp and snatch her hand back.

"It's not a good idea. See?" he said, and used a long branch to poke through the rip and instantly pull it back. The tip of the branch was charred and steaming like burning wood in the winter.

Lisa left soon after, but I stood on the doorstep watching her race back to her house with a hammering in my chest.

———

Neighbors and people I'd never even met started showing up in our backyard, even when we shooed them away. They hopped our fence, which wasn't very high, and stood in front of the rip, daring each other, even betting each other, to stick a hand, an arm, a leg, even their head through to the other side. I was at work, but when I got home for dinner Ramon said that one young kid with a mousy blond beard stuck his head through for just a second, but when he popped back out again, his beard caught fire, burning clean off his face, and his eyes were as milky as the moon on a cloudy night. He had to be taken away by ambulance, and the rest of them were much more cautious about going near the rip after that. Still, our home became a squatting ground for the curious and the down-right invasive.

Before long, the police started coming around, drawn by the traffic around our small yellow house. Ramon kept the knife wrapped and hidden in a drawer in the garage. We didn't want any excuse for the cops to harass us further. When they asked to be let into the backyard, not really asking so much as pushing open the gate and walking past us, they watched the few people crowded around the rip, looking puzzled.

"You charging money for this?" one tall blond cop asked.

"No sir. These people just keep showing up, even when we ask them not to," Ramon said.

"Well, be sure that you don't. We'll take care of this," the cop said, and he and another officer stepped over to the folks around the rip and led them away. It didn't matter. They came back the next day.

Ramon worked from home most days. He was able to guard the rip better than I was, but as I went about my days checking in patients at the clinic and entering medical records, I found myself distracted, texting him every few hours for updates. He was becoming less reliable about shuffling people out of the yard. At night I would wake up to Panda whining and the empty bed as I reached for Ramon, only to find him standing outside by the rip, listening. There were so many times when we visited his father when all he did was listen and wait for his father to tell him something loving before he died. I had never spoken with his father before the stroke. I didn't know what to listen for.

I knew I heard whispers when I stood close to the rip, but I never understood the voices. They modulated and morphed from one to many tones. He seemed to hear a more distinct voice on the other side. Sometimes he whispered, "Yes, I hear you." Once I laid my hand on his arm, he jerked out of his trance and let me lead him warily back to bed where he would kiss me senseless until we both fell asleep.

It had been a month since the rip opened. We ate dinner at the kitchen table for the first time.

"I'm worried that the police are going to come back. Or feds. Someone from the government is bound to want to take a look," I said. Ramon chewed in silence. I imagined our home becoming a militarized border with helicopters flying overhead and men in tactical gear and automatic weapons guarding the rip, crushing my wilting herb garden and tearing down the hammock where I liked to read.

"I wouldn't worry. It's our home."

"Since when has that stopped the government before?"

"I wouldn't worry," he repeated, taking another dazed bite.

I wanted to flip his plate off the table and force him to look at what I had broken. Every day took him a little further away. In the nursing home, Ramon called his father Papi and spoke so softly I could imagine him as a child. I hadn't recognized that version of Ramon, and I didn't like him either, but I wished for one moment as I stared at him across the table that I could have the meek, child-like Ramon in front of me instead of this Ramon who dreamed awake and was unreachable.

When the full moon was becoming visible, I went into the yard to water our garden and hurry off anyone who had come to visit the rip. There were five people standing with their backs to me looking up at the slight outline of the moon. Ramon was standing beside them. I tapped him on the shoulder to tell him it was time to make these people go. I saw his face, and knew that he had gone through the rip. His mouth was open in a dark, sucking *O* and his eyes were a fiery yellow and red. He raised his arms to the sky and so did the others as if they were going to take flight.

The rip began to ripple at the edges, glowing the same fiery red as Ramon's eyes. A dark gray smoke flowed from the opening, reaching out toward me like a hand searching for purchase on the nearest solid object, trying to climb out.

THAT RED SMILE

Arturo pressed the tips of his fingers along the seam of the pastel blue papel picado, letting the paste set the paper before applying another layer to the five-point star, this one a bubblegum pink. The piñata was a classic star shape with dancing fringes on the ends and gold foil points. Inside, it was hollow, waiting to be filled. He was careful with the box cutter as he surgically opened the top of the star, leaving an opening where the parents could put the dulces and other treats for their child.

Once he was finished, he hung the star from the rope attached to the ceiling through the loop at the top of the star to test its weight and balance. Arturo pushed one of the points and it wobbled a bit before spinning like an orbit. Not his best work, but pretty enough to be smashed to bits and thrown in the garbage within a week. All that could be captured is the smile of the child when they saw their piñata, when they stumble-stepped toward it, blindfolded, dizzy from being roughly spun by loving hands, and pushed toward the breaking of beautiful, fragile things.

Arturo took down the star and put it behind the counter for the woman who would be picking it up later. Around him, the shelves of his tiny shop were filled with burros, buhos, conejos, and other animales that were popular with the kids, and the gaping smiles of knock-off Elsas, Marios, Barbies and, for the adults, effigies of certain hated former presidents that they took delight in hitting when the beer flowed and the tios got going, egging each other on. It made him smile that people were still buying them.

He sat behind the counter drinking his café that was already going cold and watching cars pass by the windows. His wife Carla had packed him a volio con frijol y queso in one of her embroidered towels, but he wasn't hungry yet. There might not be anyone else in the shop until 2 PM to look around, or to pick up special orders, and it was only 11 AM now. After checking the time on his phone and taking another sip of coffee, Arturo put his glasses on and went to the worktable in the back room. Carla was always telling him to clean back here, but he liked to have all the papers, pastes, cutting tools, and decorations exploding off the shelves and at his fingertips. It did mean that he constantly had brightly colored tissue paper stuck to his shoes.

There was a shelf toward the back of the room near the bathroom where they kept a minifridge and a shelf full of cardboard boxes and other recycled materials. A piñata with the figure of a young black-haired girl in a purple dress leaned against the shelf, half-covered with a dirty white sheet. He went to take the sheet off it and pulled the piñata carefully off the shelf and set her standing on the table. The feet were perfectly balanced and did not make her wobble. Arturo stood back from the table and looked over his daughter's piñata, one that he had been working on for two months leading up to her birthday in March. He had put more time and detail into the design of the face, including her bushy black eyebrows, the way he had folded the papel to simulate her small ringlets around her shoulders, the green of her eyes. He stepped to the shelf and pulled a length of gold foil ribbon with a sweep of his arm, cutting it and wrapping it around the waist of his little girl to make a regal sash. He pasted it in place with a bow at her back.

Luisa asked for this piñata for her seventh birthday party last year, but there wasn't time. Luisa's respiratory illness worsened day by day after a seemingly mild flu infection months before. They tried Vicks, ginger teas, and running a humidifier nonstop. Even with her inhalers she wheezed and coughed constantly until the night her breaths were faint puffs and they rushed her to the hospital, though neither of them had health insurance. Luisa was immediately sedated and put on a respirator, which the doctor promised was just a precaution until her oxygen levels went up.

They had come home from the hospital one night at 2 AM, leaving Luisa behind under the care of the night shift nurses in the Pediatric ICU so that Arturo and Carla could shower and sleep for a few hours, and when they returned in the morning, Luisa's lungs were full of fluid that could no longer be drained. Their baby was drowning in her own body, fluid in her chest and around her heart. Even the machines could not save her.

Leaving the hospital without their baby felt like their reality splitting into two distinct parts, Luisa alive with them, and Luisa lowered into the ground in her best yellow church dress and somehow, they had to keep living, even though it felt like she had been cut out of the fabric of their world. The seams of his life without her were crooked, uneven, impossible to sew back together.

From a drawer, Arturo took out his Xacto knife, making a small, barely visible slice to his thumb. Blood welled to the surface, helped by a small pressure from pressing his index finger to his thumb, and Arturo swiped his thumb across Luisa's black line of a mouth, drawing a wider crimson smile. It made her look more like his living daughter, yet so alien, as though he couldn't remember

Luisa ever really existing in the first place. At least this bloody smile matched her vibrancy.

Arturo liked piñata Luisa's smile.

When Arturo came back in the morning, the Luisa piñata was standing on the worktable in the back room. He set down his keys on the steel tabletop and moved closer to the piñata. Along the seam of one arm, the papel was flat, the pink and lavender and pastel blue blending together into a thin skin. Arturo ran his thumb along this smooth patch, like the hairless skin of a baby.

Later, when Carla came by the store to bring him lunch and the tax receipts she'd been entering for the last two months, she found him in the back room with their daughter's effigy staring back with its unreal smile.

"Has anyone come in this morning?"

"Two people."

"You have a special order for Friday, three piñatas. Did you forget?"

"The first one is easy, we already have a dog, I just need to change its outfit. I'll work on the other two shortly."

Arturo picked Luisa up and put her back on the shelf. His wife touched his shoulder where she had endless times before. He turned, giving her a weak smile, then returned to the task of adding a blue tutu to a brown dog piñata. Easy work.

The bloody smile of the Luisa piñata had faded into a coral pink. She appeared on the worktable every morning. When Arturo went to pick her up, new patches of papel picado had transformed into smooth skin. Her limbs, at first sticking out straight and rigid, were now bent and thrust forward like they were reaching to be picked up. Luisa used to jump into his arms just like that.

Arturo picked her up, hugged her to his chest. He hoped Carla didn't catch him in the middle of this embrace. Against his chest, he swore there was a faint heart beating against his own. He held the Luisa piñata away from him and watched as her blood mouth pulsed against the paper like she was bursting to open her mouth and speak to him. Arturo found himself reaching for the Xacto knife again and running it along the bloody line of her mouth. The paper parted into an opening that puffed out air in a gentle sigh. More noise came from the hole, a throat clinging to a barely there voice.

"¿Que quieres mi niña? What do you want to say?"

More faint whistles and moans, but still sound emanating from that seemingly hollow little body. Arturo brough the Luisa piñata to the front of the store with him while he organized papers and entered new receipts into their ancient Mac computer, squinting at the numbers, while he swept, and when he went to the workroom on her little stool she used to sit on as he finished work on a three-tiered pink and white cake piñata with yellow candles that someone was picking up later that day. The more he moved her around with him, following him as she used to on weekends when she would help him at the store, those noises from her bloody little mouth took form, became more distinct. Between bites of his ham and cheese sandwich with lettuce and tomato from their home garden, Arturo swore the Luisa piñata murmured, "Papi please."

Arturo pinched off pieces of his sandwich. Tenderly, he pushed them into the hole of Luisa's new mouth, thinking how silly he was to feed a hollow box of paper and glue, until he heard her pleased hums when he brought his fingers to her lips. The last little piece he pushed in disappeared, but the Luisa piñata's mouth closed over his finger, nipping him and drawing a few drops of bright blood. He pulled his hand back, stung by her insistence and her hunger. Still, he saw how feeding her allowed more movement in her limbs, and the flimsy waves of her paper hair to solidify into more distinct strands.

It pained him to close up that night, leaving the Luisa piñata on the shelf. Instead, he made a little nest for her on the torn sofa in the workroom, pulling paint-stained t-shirts and newspapers together to cover her. He would have taken her home, all of him was straining to carry her to his car and buckle her in the back seat as he always had, but Carla. He hadn't shown her to Carla yet. There was an impulse to keep this closed up in his heart a little longer. Arturo left one of the back lights on for the Luisa piñata so she wouldn't be scared.

The last drops of blood Luisa took from Arturo fed her, but now there was a change happening to him, too. He woke to angry red rashes up and down his arms. When he scrubbed, his thick black hair fell out into the sink in curlicues and skin flaked off like wet paper. Carla rubbed aloe from their garden onto his arms to sooth them though the throbbing pain had already subsided. Now it was centered on his stomach.

"¿Te llevo a la clinica?" The same worry he saw in her eyes when Luisa was in the hospital was bright in Carla's eyes now.

"It's nothing. Just some indigestion."

Carla still made him drink a sickly sweet Pedialite in the morning. He stopped drinking his morning coffee as his stomach burned and gurgled inside. In the bathroom, he coughed up bright blue and yellow papel picado and flushed them away.

The Luisa piñata talked more frequently now, and when

Arturo's stomach pain was sharp and insistent, he locked the door to the store and sat in the workroom with her, reading one of her favorite books she used to love and letting her run her rough little hands along his hairless arms. She had formed separate fingers from the cardboard that tickled as they touched him. He brought his stiff finger to her mouth, allowing her to suckle the blood—his daily tithe, when the front door opened and Carla shuffled in calling for Arturo and demanding to know why the front door was closed when the store should have been open.

She stopped in the doorway to the workroom, watching her husband feed the lifelike Luisa piñata.

"Amor..." he whispered.

Carla moved toward them slowly, letting her black purse slip from her shoulder onto the floor, her keys falling from her hand with a clang against the concrete. Arturo withdrew his finger from Luisa's mouth like he'd been caught doing something unholy. Luisa rotated her piñata body, more fluid now than it had ever been, toward her mother.

"Mami!" she said, lifting her arms to be picked up as though months had not passed since they watched her heart stop and buried her in her yellow dress. Carla's face crumpled like tissue paper smashed in a person's hand. She moved to Luisa and picked her up, hugging her close. The Luisa piñata was heavier, carried more weight the longer she was alive in this world.

Carla sobbed into Luisa's hair, wetting the dye on her dress and making the colors run like the watercolor paintings they used to do with Luisa on Sundays.

"Mi niña. Mi preciosa," Carla whispered again and again, rocking Luisa back and forth. Arturo came to her and together they held their piñata daughter close.

The more lifelike Luisa grew, the more Arturo's stomach burned. Most days it took him an hour just to get out of bed. He knew he had to keep feeding her with his life's blood, but every day more hair fell out, his skin thinning and bruising, his stomach and chest boiling with insistence. Carla cared for Luisa more and more as Arturo could not, and sometimes he missed having their daughter to himself.

When he got to the store that morning, the front door was open and Carla was in the workroom whispering and laughing with Luisa, the sound so familiar it made Arturo dizzy with longing for a time without interruptions, without the loss of their child. Arturo snuck in, not wanting to intrude, and went to his tool shelf to take out the exacto knife. His fingertips were sore from the small slices he had made to bring his daughter back to life.

"Papi, I don't need it today," Luisa said. She was able to sit on the metal tabletop and swing her legs, no longer rigid.

"Are you sure amor? What will you eat now?" Carla went to the other side of the room to get something out of the closet.

"I don't need your blood anymore," she said, those legs kicking faster, swish-swishing the paper of her dress. "I need you."

Arturo held the metal table for support. Lightning pain flashed through his stomach and chest.

"Please Papi, I need you to do this for me!" Luisa screeched. Her skin had become a mixture of papel and thin brown patches across her face and arms. Her purple dress ruffled and flowed in her anger, more real fabric than paper. Her hair puffed out around her head, the dark strands more distinctive now as though an electrical storm was blowing in. Scraps of paper, ribbons, and fabric swirled around the room and the lights above flickered violently.

"Mi amor, I would do anything for you, but how can we be together if you do this?"

"I'm not doing it. Mami is," said Luisa, and her paper smile ripped her mouth open wide as she turned toward her mother standing next to the table in the corner. Carla held up the broken broom handle out of the mop bucket, ready to swing.

She moved toward her husband, Luisa watching gleefully, and brought the mop handle back. Carla swung the bat toward Arturo's stomach, hitting him hard enough that the air left him in a *whoosh*, and his stomach burst open in an explosion of rainbow papel that blanketed the room. Arturo hit the floor, papel and blood seeping out of the enormous hole in his stomach. Luisa jumped gleefully off the table and knelt by her father who gasped for air with a hollow chest. She reached into the hole of his stomach, up past his ribcage and tore out his tie-dyed heart. Arturo's last thought was how vibrant she looked as she bit into its weeping, wet pulp.

LET MOMMY REST...

That's what Dad told me whenever I sat crossed legged outside of their bedroom, never letting my bare feet slip across the light wood grain of the threshold. From where I sat, I couldn't see Mommy's body or her deep rising chest. It looked like she had sunk so deep into the mattress, under the covers, that her body disappeared completely.

Mommy has aches. They start in her head, where her hair meets her face, and travel down like lightning strikes to the tips of her toes. She takes medicine for it, and most days she moves slow but she can do things like make us breakfast, fold the laundry (with my help) and take me to school before she goes to work at the library. But these days, her bad days, Daddy tells me not to bother Mommy.

But I don't want to bother her. I want to climb up on the bed and help change the cold washcloths she puts over her eyes when the aches get bad. I want to rub the shocks out of her feet while we watch TV in the dark, so quiet I can barely hear it. I want to read her a book, one she knows so she doesn't have to follow along, or a new one she brought home from work that she needs to read for the next Librarians Recommend display. I want to help, just like she helps me when I feel sick or when I don't want to get out of bed. Dad says to leave her alone, so I do.

Dad's at work today. I don't have school on Fridays, so I get to sit in the warm cocoon of my blankets staring up at the stars on my ceiling. They glow and shimmer in the dark.

Before he left, Dad came in to give me a hug and to have a good day. He reminded me that today is a Mommy rest day, a "bad pain day," as she calls it, and that I should try to do what I can to leave her be.

"I made oatmeal and granola for breakfast and left you a sandwich and apple slices in the fridge for lunch. You can watch TV for a little while, but not too long, okay?"

I agree, still in that warm lovely place where sleep holds me close.

"I love you baby. See you later when I get home."

Normally on Fridays, I get to go to work with Mommy. She makes us eggs on toast or blueberry pancakes and lets me help her carry her big backpack and boxes of books or activities she is going to set out in the kids' section, with my help. I look forward to Fridays.

It seems like Mommy has her bad pain days more and more now.

This morning, I finally wriggle out of bed and shuffle downstairs to get the oatmeal that Dad made me from the fridge. I mix in more milk and put it in the microwave for a minute, then add cinnamon and a little honey, maybe too much because some spills onto the countertop and my hands feel sticky even after I finish eating. I haven't heard any noises from Mommy yet, so I go back upstairs and knock on her door. Maybe she is hungry now and ready to eat.

"Mommy? Dad left us oatmeal if you want some for breakfast. Or I can make you some tea."

No sounds on the other side. I sit cross legged on the floor and wait. Still nothing, so I decide to go downstairs to the kitchen again and use the step stool Dad leaves for me to get Mommy's "World's Best Librarian" mug from the cabinet and put a tea bag in it for her. Then I fill the kettle a little and turn on the stove (Dad doesn't like me to do this when no one is there to help, but I know how to do it without letting the flame get too high). The kettle starts steaming and whistling, so I pour the water over the tea bag and dunk it down with a spoon like Mommy showed me, adding honey in there too. Now my hands are really sticky. I almost forget to turn off the stove, even though Dad always reminds me that's very important.

Carefully, I hold the steaming mug in both hands as I climb the stairs again, placing one foot in front of the other very slowly.

"Mommy?"

I knock again.

"I made you some tea."

Still no sound on the other side. A prickly feeling runs along my forehead. I'm feeling annoyed, but remember that Dad said to leave Mommy be, so I leave the tea outside the door for her and go back to my room.

I read one of my new longer chapter books about a witch and a mermaid who become pirates and sail the seven seas. Then I stretch, turn on some music to dance around, pick up clothes off the floor to put away for laundry, draw at my desk in my blue notebook, and when I still haven't heard anything from Mommy's room, I return to the hallway. The mug of tea is still sitting outside her door, the water cold and brown.

Something slithers in my stomach. I knock on the door again.

"Mommy, are you awake?"

On the other side of the door, I hear a fizzling, sizzling noise like when Dad cooks bacon on the griddle.

The sound gets louder, followed by some thumps like meat hitting the floor.

"Mom? Mommy, are you okay?"

I open the door a crack to peer inside.

Mommy's body is not solid anymore. I climb over the side of the sinking, stinking mattress. Where her body had been is a gooey, slippery layer of what I think used to be her skin. It looks like an egg that was cracked open too hard against the pan and broke open. In the middle, where her insides should be, is a dark hole in the mattress like something burned straight through it. I don't want to touch it with my bare hands, it looks like it would eat away my skin, so I take the backscratcher I sometimes use on Dad's back and poke it into the sticky hole.

Underneath the bed, the mattress swells up, taking a breath. I scramble off and watch it rise again and start to shake.

The mattress flips across the room with a bang so fast I can barely get out of the way in time. Something rises to its feet. Its eyes are yellow and red, bulging from its head under brows like cliffs over brown, moist skin, somehow both scaly and furry. It stretches up so high its head hits the ceiling, short amber-colored horns scraping some of the paint off.

I breathe in a shudder and try to crab walk backward across the hardwood floor but the thing that is Mommy hears me, turns in my direction and growls. Lips peel back over yellowed fangs, viscous goo sliding down the sides of her face. There is so much to look at, my eyes can't focus on one feature of her new face. I slide backward over the rug until my butt is across the doorway and I am scooting to the stairs. Hulking steps follow. When I am almost on the stairs, the creature that is now Mommy emerges from the room. It's time to run.

My feet slip on the wood of the stairs. I feel a nail catch and rip on my big toe but I keep running because the Mommy creature claws and leaps across the wooden floor after me. I don't have a plan, but if I can get downstairs, I might be able to lock myself into the closet. I throw myself down the rest of the steps and hurtle full speed into the closet, hitting my head on the back wall before slamming the door shut. It rattles with the force of the Mommy creature once, twice, and then it stops. The shadow of her casts across the doorframe, her claws clicking against the floor.

I sit back in the coats hanging around me in the stink of over-worn shoes and rock back and forth as Mommy slams against the door again and again.

What does she want?

The door splinters. Mommy leans her hulking fanged head inside so close her spit drips across my knees. She reaches a claw toward my neck. I squeeze my eyes shut, so scared I feel sick but still wishing I could make sure she is okay.

"Mommy please."

Her claw cuts into my cheek. She scoops my blood to her gaping mouth, licks it from her claws, sniffs and lets it fall over her tongue. That claw reaches back to my face. I am sure that those eyes are the last thing I am going to see. Instead, she strokes my bleeding skin. Her claw is surprisingly warm.

In her old body, Mommy was a big hugger. She had a squishy belly and arms that would wrap me up in a cinnamon-smelling swirl. Mommy creature doesn't smell good now, but the way she nuzzles is still comforting, even if she leaves a trail of sticky goo on my face like a wet kiss.

Just as I start to wonder what Mommy creature would be hungry for—she hasn't eaten all day—keys scrape against the lock of the front door and I hear Dad stepping in, wiping his shoes on the doormat, calling me to come help him with the pizza he brought home for a late lunch.

"C'mon Mommy." I take her clawed, dripping paw. "Let's go eat."

WISHING YOU THE BEST

Weeks after the surgery, I was still finding flowers on my body. A sickly butter yellow daisy was wound through my curls, a bluebell in the crease of my stomach, a chrysanthemum braided into the hair of my armpit. My first gentle shower sent petals cascading down the drain.

After my surgery, I received a card in the mail from my care team. Sky-blue wildflowers were embossed across the front of the card. Flipping the card open, I read a generic printed message from my surgeon and the nursing team: "We wish you the best in your recovery!"

The worst part of surgery was what I couldn't remember. Anesthesia rhymes with amnesia for a reason.

I pinned the card to the fridge. When I looked at it too long, the flowers bled like watercolors in my vision. Maybe it was time for another pain pill. I still had a month before the sutures were supposed to be removed but I could barely keep food down. At night I dreamed water flowed from my wound, cascading down my belly like a river carving through stone.

At home I cleaned the suture lines that ran across my belly. The wound itched as it was healing, and I cleaned it with a gentle antibacterial soap. Looking at the wound in the mirror where skin was stitched to skin, pops of green stems poked through. I wiggled my finger into the wound, popping open the skin. An array of flowers spilled forth, a bouquet falling from my stomach.

CURATIVE

Never let them turn your eyes, my love, or bite off your tongue from the root

Never cry tears just so they may have salt for their tables

Take out the copper pot, yes, that one with the burned bottom best for stewing

Turn the heat on high, high, higher, it should feel like your hand will catch fire when you hold it over the pot. Yes, good, you want the air smoking

Now, let me open myself up

Hush girl, no need for that, it doesn't hurt, see how the cut is already closing up? It has to be the chest, over the heart where everything is most potent

This isn't just blood, look how dark it is

It's the things we remember in our bones

All the fearsome care, the whispers over the stove when we

knew they weren't listening, the wounds tended to, the freefall of despair, the hopes we sewed up into our skin just for you

Pour it now, into the pot but mind the splatter
Now, turn down the heat to let it simmer
Don't worry if you start to hear screaming
Add some of that fresh rosemary you picked from the garden, so fragrant just off the stem, a little lemon juice and a dollop of honey to thicken it, makes it sweeter too
Turn off the heat and let it cool
See now, it doesn't look so bad now, does it? A fragrant pink tincture perfect for this little vial. Don't spill a drop!
You can pour this into your tea to cut the bitter herbs, use it as a syrup, even dribble it across your lover's back
Just trust, it will soothe what ails you deep down inside

YOU DON'T GO WHERE
YOU DON'T GROW

There were always reasons not to go home, but Laura was running out of them. Laura's mother called her after she fell in the kitchen and bruised her hip badly enough to go to the minor emergency clinic in town, thirty minutes from her house. Her mother lived alone and Laura was her only child. Need came calling, even when you were at your limits.

Her partner Allan helped her pack an overnight bag for her stay. After this third miscarriage, they knew how to maneuver around each other like their bodies were too scalded with grief to let their skins touch. Laura knew that his grieving was more private, something he hid away from her with his care as her body expelled their almost baby. Her body didn't give up these pregnancies easily. Was pain that was expected easier to swallow? Maybe for him, and Laura felt a little ashamed of that, but all she wanted to do each time someone asked how she was doing was to reach a hand between her bloodied legs and wipe a bloody handprint across their face in a cackle.

On the way to her mother's house, Laura stopped at a drugstore off I-35 North. She filled a basket with Corn Nuts, an iced tea, and picked out a medical-grade cane with a strong rubber grip. Her mother was probably hobbling around the house using her hands for balance against the cabinets and walls. At the self-checkout, the machine wouldn't scan the barcode on the cane. An employee came around the counter begrudgingly to help, making Laura raise the cane in the air to hand to him and, for a moment, he reared back like she was going to hit him with it. A surge of violence swelled in her; if only she could take out her anger on this unsuspecting boy and bring her mother a blood splattered cane as an offering of goodwill. Her mother loved horror movies, the more violent the better, so maybe she would understand.

As she paid for her snacks and the cane, Laura looked into the security camera footage of her own face, briefly distorted and wavy before her face came back into focus. That sometimes happened. Photos of her didn't always develop properly. Her very spiritual friend Michelle told her that her aura was just too strong to be captured on film. It felt right now when her body had betrayed her, when she didn't recognize her own face.

The gravel driveway to the old house was short. The property was only a few acres now since the Gomez family had sold off the rest of the West Texas ranch long before. At the gate there was a sign that read "Rancho Perdido." It made the place sound both mysterious and like a paradise, though all land here was touched by dispossession and violence. She didn't know who in the family had named the property; that sign had hung there as long as she had been alive. Tio Hector had taken to calling it "the last place." Since he'd moved to California, it was just the last place he wanted to be.

Laura got out, leaving the car idling, and punched in the combination for the lock that chained the gate, thinking that if her mother ever had a real emergency and couldn't get up, she was doomed. No one would be able to get to her unless they had bolt cutters. That thought made it hard for Laura to breathe for a few seconds. She drove a little way through the gate, then got out and locked it again behind her as her mother always asked her to do. Driving up, her mother waved at her from the porch where she sat on the short white wicker swing, its cushion covered in a millennia of dog hair from their mutt Chiquita, who was anything but. The bristly gray and white dog met Laura at her car door, wanting to jump up and slobber on her jeans before she was even out of the car.

"Hi Chiquita, hello hello! Get down now." Laura pat her head and simultaneously pushed her down so she could exit the car without tripping. Laura's heartbeat quickened pace seeing her mother's calm face. She was dreading telling her the news, but there was a desperation there too, below her skin, that needed her mother's gentle touch and unflinching eyes.

"Hi Mom." Laura leaned down to kiss her mother on the cheek and sat next to her, making the porch swing sway a little. Her mother had her silvering black hair piled on top of her head in a messy bun. She wore white loose cotton shorts and a sage tank top, appearing so effortlessly comfortable, something that Laura had always admired. Sitting next to her mother, Laura noticed how her light brown skin had deepened, become more sundrenched, but there was also a mottled bruise on her thigh and more raised purple veins that hadn't been there before. Laura reached for the bruise, but her mother pulled away and crossed her legs.

"That looks bad," Laura said. Her mother shrugged.

"Doesn't even hurt anymore, just a little tender. You know me, I'm thick skinned."

"Hmmm," Laura agreed, stretching her arm around her mother's shoulder.

"I'm glad you're staying over," her mother conceded, smiling at her daughter as Chiquita tried in vain to jump onto the wobbly porch swing in between them. "Allan didn't want to come and see me?" Her mother liked Allan and his sweet, thoughtful quietness, so different from the two women and their loud, prickly personalities, especially when they got to drinking and carrying on. Maybe that was the way to get out this loss, and introduce the cane to her mother, once she broke open the two bottles of wine she had in the paper grocery bags in the back of the car.

"Allan had to finish a training for work. Besides, he wanted us to have some time."

Laura's mother looked sideways at her, tilting her chin up and lowering her thinning eyebrows, not with suspicion but with an unspoken understanding that something needed saying.

"That's fine. Just us girls then," she said, scratching Chiquita behind the ear with her toes painted with chipped peach polish.

"I'll go bring some things in from the car and we can get dinner started. I brought that wine you liked the last time, from the vineyard in Blanco." Her mother's eyes went mischief dark and she slapped Laura's knee.

"Ok, I see it's gonna be that kind of party!"

When it got dark, Laura spooned an extra heap of mushroom pasta onto her plate and poured a generous portion of the red blend into two glasses. Her mother had put up little lantern lights around the porch and lit a candle for the mosquitos persisting even into October. They slurped the spaghetti, cream sauce hanging on to the corners of their lips, and screeched into the dark.

"I haven't gotten tipsy like this in a while." Laura leaned her head back onto the swing where she could see the stars more clearly than in the city.

"Me either. You want a little more?" And without waiting for an answer, her mother pulled out a clear bottle of mezcal with no label and a blue ribbon tied around the neck like a royal gift.

"Is that man still giving you free booze?!" Laura laughed while her mother uncorked the bottle and giggled.

"It's his business! Don Juanito is nice!"

"Hmmm, I'm sure he is."

Her mother took a shallow swig from the bottle, smacking her lips at the burn, and passed it to her daughter who took a longer pull and spit directly into the air, a spray of acrid droplets raining down on them.

"Hey! Don't waste the good stuff," her mother laughed, wiping her face and taking the bottle back. Maybe when she was younger, Laura's lack of impulse control would have bothered her, mainly in times when it embarrassed her mother, like when she interrupted her conversations on the phone or did cartwheels in public, but as she got older, it seemed to Laura that her mother's sense of propriety and shame melted away with age, a second skin being cast off the fewer fucks she gave.

Warmth settled over Laura's body, one she had missed in the months before learning she was pregnant. Her body felt smooth and pliant, and even the residual cramping in her pelvis was like an afterthought.

It had been three weeks. She'd taken off two days to schedule time at home to induce the miscarriage. Laura was given a kit to preserve the fetal remains so that her doctor could send them off for genetic testing to determine if a chromosomal abnormality was at the center of this loss too, or her sticky, wanting womb. As she opened the box and prepared the sterile cup, she noticed that the back of the box was labeled "exempt human remains." Her baby was exempt from humanity for never growing past the sixth week, and yet she was being asked to collect their remains like collecting evidence at a crime scene. When the worst of the bleeding started, Laura squatted over the toilet, her legs shaking from the effort and her arms covered in cold sweat while cramp after cramp rode through her belly, and held the cup close to her body to capture the dark bloody clump that was the placenta, the fetal tissue. What was one more traumatic act in the scheme of things, one more loss like deep violent notches in the tree of her heart?

"Mom, I need to tell you something."

Her mother looked at her, not with surprise or fear, but a patient neutrality that Laura cherished right now. Laura realized her hands were shaking.

"I found out I was pregnant a couple of months ago. We had our first scan, and the doctor told us the bad news. I already took the meds to take care of things, but I may have to have an additional surgery." There was gratitude in Laura as her throat felt like it was shutting for good, that her mother had been there the last two times to care for her in her own quiet way.

"Ok baby. Thank you for telling me. How are you feeling?"

Laura squeezed her burning eyes up tight. She hadn't cried at the doctor's office or at home with Allan holding her on the sofa, not even when she felt their baby slip out of her body and into the sterile plastic cup. Something about her mother calling her *baby*, seeing her still as a baby, not just as a woman whose body had failed yet again, brought the tears up and overflowing and Laura choked into the humid night air.

"I'm okay. It still hurts, but things are healing. We'll see."

Her mother thrust the heavy bottle of mezcal back at her daughter and Laura let clear liquor burn her tears away.

In the morning, Laura drank black coffee on the porch while her mother limped outside to join her. She produced the cane she had been waiting to gift her.

"I got this for you. I think it will really help."

Her mother didn't take the cane. She walked around Laura's feet, making a point to step high like her physical therapist had instructed, a prancing walk like a strutting pony. She settled on the cushioned chair next to the porch swing and threw up her hands in a "ta da!" pose.

"I'm leaving it for you here whether you use it or not." Laura leaned the cane against the wall between them. She wanted to yell at her mother to take this offering, though an offering could never be forced.

"I can run the mower today. And refill the bird feeders," Laura offered.

Her mother sipped some coffee and nodded. "If you want to."

Laura rolled her eyes.

While it was still cool, Laura rode around on the John Deere riding lawnmower across the few acres of field surrounding the house, cutting down the grass to a walkable height. Rattlesnakes hid in the long grass in summer, another of Laura's fears for when her mother was alone here. There were a few nearby neighbors, Don Juanito for instance, but even still, it had taken over an hour for her mother to be able to get up after her fall and drive herself to the clinic. A snakebite would take a lot less time to incapacitate her.

When Laura was done mowing, sweating through her t-shirt, she went inside for water and ate two ham sandwiches before she helped her mother refill the bird feeders around the house. Laura filled each with birdseed and shook the feed down so that the tray was full for the cardinals, sparrows, and gray doves that nested nearby. They called all day, but for some reason as soon as Laura stepped into the canopy of trees, on the little dirt path to the creek behind the house, the sound became more muffled.

Every time she looked at the well-worn path, even now, it loomed before her, and Laura's vision blurred like she was staring down an endless hallway that pulsed with a beating heart.

When Laura was a kid, her mother wasn't overly strict like some of her friends' parents. Laura could play at her friends' houses on the weekends if they didn't live too far away, and if Laura finished her homework beforehand. For most of her life, it was just the two of them together. They learned that they had to trust each other to care for each other, and Laura never questioned learning early on how to make her own lunch, start simple dinners when her mother worked late, to do chores around the property. It was just what needed to be done.

The only times her mother would get upset were when she didn't know where Laura was for longer than a couple of hours. She didn't like Laura to walk home on the country road to their house alone, as the eighteen-wheelers took turns too fast. She made sure to meet all her friends' parents so she would know who Laura was hanging out with. And when Laura's friends came over to the ranch, they could play anywhere but in the creek. Her mother went on about the bacteria, viruses borne by mosquitos, and not wanting to be responsible for one of her friends getting hurt or even drowning.

Laura's best friend Emma lived down the road from them. She was obsessed with fairy books and claimed that the path lined with wildflowers after spring rain was the path to a fairy ring by the creek where several live oaks and cypress trees surrounded the water. When Laura's mother was busy at the house folding laundry and doing other chores, Laura and Emma would follow that path to the creek. They built a table of water-smoothed rocks to leave offerings of bright yellow dandelions, apple juice in a chipped mug, and Oreos, because Emma said fairies liked sweet things to eat.

The last time they visited their fairy altar the weather was humid, and Emma decided to strip off her pink socks and wade halfway into the creek, her ankles and toes translucent white in the clear green water. Laura was taking off her shoes and rolling off her sweaty socks to join her when she heard her mother yelling for them to come in for lunch. Emma's legs were wet, and her mother sent Emma home early and Laura to her room for the rest of the night. Her mother didn't yell. Her silence was a disappointed barrier between her and Laura that always communicated when Laura had messed up. She'd gone back into the woods since then, but never took anyone to the creek again. The fairy altar was left abandoned.

The green canopy above Laura's head let in bright dappled light. Laura walked barefoot through the grass, stopping to touch the butter-yellow flowers along the path, each grasping sticky blade of grass, and let the grasshoppers fly past her as she made her way toward the shade of the creek behind her mother's house. At the bank of the creek there was a wicker basket with a blanket tucked around a bundle like a fresh loaf of bread. Even in the dream, Laura felt a knowing unease about throwing back the blanket, but her hand reached out and unwrapped the bundle.

Underneath, a baby Laura didn't recognize squirmed and scrunched their face. Their skin was the color of Laura's mother's and their head was covered in glossy whisps of black hair. Laura reached for the baby to pick them up but the baby cried a cry that reverberated across the canopy of trees. The baby's skin began to ripple and quake, dissolving before her eyes into moist sand and grit slipping through Laura's hands.

When she woke, Laura's hands were wet with grit and she sat up in bed to sob, a deep rhythm finding her body. She'd dreamt of her lost babies before, imagined them living, but being home made the dream more vivid, the technicolor of the woods more vibrant. Being back home wasn't always a comfort.

Laura shut a whining Chiquita out of her room and took a scalding shower, then called Allan, just to check in. She thought she would enjoy these few days away from him and their collective hurt, but she found herself missing the deep, soothing sound of his voice near her ear.

"How's it going?" he asked, as though her grief was a project she was working on.

"It's fine. Mom misses you. How did you become her favorite?"

Allan's deep chuckle echoed through the phone. Laura loved to feel the vibration of that sound, of his lips, against the back of her neck.

"I'm just that charming, she doesn't even mind if I'm pocho and can't speak Spanish too well."

"Nombre, she's pocha too, just doesn't like anyone telling her that," Laura laughed, then settled into her serious voice. "I told her."

"And how did that go?"

Laura thought about it. "I think as well as it could. It wasn't a long conversation, but I felt like she heard me. I mean, it was less what she said but that she knew, you know?"

She could hear Allan shuffling around the house as they talked, probably trying to clean up her mess while she was gone.

"I'm glad, babe. It's important. She knows what this has been like for you."

"For us," Laura returned. Sometimes she needed to remind herself that it was both of them feeling disappointment and anger that they let themselves hope in the first place, though it was her body bearing the brunt of this suffering.

"Yes, but what I mean is she went through this too."

"Yes, that's true."

Yet Laura hadn't known about her mother's miscarriages until after she herself had had one of her own. After Laura's first D&C, her mother stayed with them for a few days. In a quiet moment when Laura was lying on the couch staring at the ceiling fan whirring as the TV played daytime talk shows in the background, her mother sat down with her, clearing her throat before she told her that she understood how Laura was feeling. Laura didn't look at her, couldn't look at her, only kept her eyes, which fogged over with stinging tears, trained on the ceiling fan's circulation. Her mother described how she had lost a few pregnancies before having Laura, her "rainbow baby." That's what they called them on the pregnancy loss support blogs and social media pages. Laura hated that term, as if all one needed to do to find their living baby was to travel to the end of a rainbow.

It was cold enough for a small fire after sunset. Dry oak and pecan logs Laura's mother had been saving since the summer cracked and spit embers into the smoky air around the fire pit. In the dark beyond the tree line, coyotes yipped, crying like ghostly spirits in the night.

"Seems like they get closer every year," Laura said, sipping from the blackberry wine her mother always liked, and who had an equally full glass that glinted in the firelight. They had moved the rocking chairs off the porch to set around the fire, and draped thick quilts around themselves after a dinner of small skirt steaks over the grill and baked potatoes loaded with butter and cheese. Laura felt pleasantly warm, full, fuzzy with wine and rocking toward the flames.

"Yes, but they know not to come too close. I still have the .22 upstairs, and besides, I have Chiquita here to guard me."

Her mother patted the wagging dog's head. She had been slipping Chiquita pieces of charred meat from the grill. Laura looked over at her mother, rocking slowly. She couldn't tell if it was comforting to know her mother still had the rifle upstairs or frightening. She had been living alone for so many years, Laura took her safety for granted, until this fall. Her mother had needs now that Laura didn't yet know how to provide for, but she would have to get wise soon to acclimate her mother to accepting help.

"Does Tio Hector still come around to help you out?"

Her mother chuckled into her wine glass. "He comes around once a year to 'check in on me' and beg for cash. He's still my baby brother at the end of it all."

"I guess that makes sense. It's nice to be here, with you," Laura told her while she turned the log in the fire that sprayed sparks into the air.

"I think so too," her mother agreed.

"I'll try to come around a bit more, when we can," Laura promised, hoping that she meant it.

"When you can."

"I guess I should get used to the idea that this will be my home again when I get older."

Her mother stared hard into the firelight.

"You and Allan have your lives. There's no expectation you give that up for me."

Laura breathed deep and nodded, though she wasn't sure if her mother could see her shadowed face. She often felt that she never visited enough, never called or texted enough, but what was a promise if not a loving lie?

Chiquita came around to sniff Laura's hand for meat residue and get scritches behind her ever-soft ears. Laura patted her and rocked into a rhythm answered by her mother's own chair rocking. It had been just them for a long time, and they found that rhythm again so easily.

Stars emerged above the canopy of oak trees, constellations Laura hadn't been able to see and name in a long while. Her neck grew stiff from staring into the black abyss of sky overtaken by bright bursts of light. For a time, she could lose sense of her own body imagining she was floating in that wide sky with nowhere to go but beyond, and nothing to be afraid of.

In the morning there was blood in Laura's underwear. The doctor told her there would be for a while, and then she should expect more when her period returned. The last of the pregnancy hormones had dwindled from her body into decimal points she read from lab results on her patient portal app. Laura's breath came in short gasps, her chest felt like it was imploding, she sank to the carpeted floor by the bed, clutching her stomach. This was her old room, and though most of her books and furniture were gone, the faded pink carpet was the same. How many times had she cried here over things that felt world rending at the time and now seemed like they were moments in another person's life?

Laura wanted to rip out her own scalding heart and hand it off to someone, to her mother, to Allan, to anyone who could stand to touch it, but there was no one who could hold that pain for her, so she sobbed until she choked and gagged on the bedroom carpet, her limbs seizing and shaking.

Her mother came hobbling into the room and sat on the bed. Her knee wouldn't allow her to bend to the floor easily, but she could sit on the edge of the bed and stroke Laura's sweaty head.

"I really thought that maybe it would happen this time. I really wanted to meet this baby."

"I know."

"Yes, but it's different. You didn't even know we were trying again."

Her mother shook her head.

"No, I mean I know."

"What do you mean?"

Her mother winced but slid to the floor next to Laura, taking Laura's hands in a surprising grip and pulling her daughter to face her.

"I lost five pregnancies, one after the other. It made me very sick, and your father didn't want to try anymore. That's when he left."

Laura stared at her mother. She knew her parents had had trouble getting pregnant, that her father was not really a father, just a man who left and was not in her life. It was always just the two of them together here. Hearing her mother talk about her own losses, five losses, Laura wondered whether she had that much strength in her to withstand that many.

"The last time, I didn't know what else to do. The placenta, this red floating moon, was in the toilet, and for some reason, I couldn't bear to flush it away. So I scooped it up in my hands and walked to the edge of the creek in the dark. I buried the placenta in some wet loose earth and scooped creek water over it to help it grow."

"Mom, why are you telling me this?" Laura's eyes were brimming over, for herself, for her mother's own pain, but her mother didn't cry, didn't look like she was telling a sad story. Instead, she looked out the window like she was speaking a secret out loud she'd promised never to tell. Her long hair was loose and hanging around the shoulders of her flowing white nightdress, and when she grabbed her daughter by the shoulders, Laura winced in pain.

"You have to listen! It's my fault this is happening to you. When I buried that piece of me, that piece of you, something decided to let you grow. When I came back to the creek in the morning, a little baby with dirt in its eyes was squirming around in a crib of brambles. I didn't ask, I didn't question, I just took you home and cleaned you up and hoped that the tierra would let me love you. I wanted you so badly, and I thought that what was given to me would be enough to mean you could have a good life.

"I was afraid that one day the land would decide to take you back. I couldn't let it take you from me," her mother said, pressing her hand down hard on Laura's still healing womb like she wanted to reach inside of Laura, "but nothing can grow here. Nothing can grow from earth and wood and stone."

"Jesus Mom." Laura squirmed away from the insistent pressure of her mother's hand on her belly. She stood up and looked down at her mother, the person who cared for her all her life. Were these the first signs of her slipping away, first the fall, then this story?

"I walked by that creek so many times, Mom, and nothing ever happened. What happened to me," Laura said, swallowing the lump rising in her throat, "it isn't your fault or mine. It just happens, you know that. And I'll show you, there is nothing to be afraid of."

Laura stood and walked downstairs and straight out the front door, down the porch steps and onto the trail that wound around to the back of the house down to the creek. The tall grass was yellowed from drought and grasped at her pajamas, but the landscape became more verdant the farther into the woods she went. Behind her, Laura heard her mother tripping after her and yelling her name. It made her smile to hear the muffled pressure of the new cane against the wooden deck.

By the time Laura reached the creek she was rolling the legs of her jeans up to her calves and submerging her feet in the clear running water. She let her toes roll over the smooth rocks of the creek bed and closed her eyes as warm sunlight bathed her face. She'd forgotten how beautiful it was back here, and how much she'd wished as a child to do just what she was doing now, like the wild girls adventuring in her favorite books.

Her mother's screams echoed across the trees and Laura watched her using the cane to furiously stomp through the grass, waving to Laura to get out of the water.

"Mom, it's okay. I'm fine."

When her mother was within ten feet of her, Laura could see tears streaming down her mother's face, trapped in the lines under her eyes and around her mouth. There was pleasure in seeing this frantic, broken side of her mother, and some secret part of Laura reveled in her mother's distress, wishing it had come sooner when Laura really needed them to break apart together.

A tingling sensation started to grow in her toes, and when Laura looked down at her feet. Dirt and sand covered them. Laura thought she had kicked some up from the creek bed, so she shifted from foot to foot. Her toes were gone. Her feet were not solid anymore. They were dissolving beneath her.

Laura yelped, wobbling violently, and fell forward on her hands and knees. Her hands stung from the rocks beneath her and the tingling began in her fingernails just as her hands began to dissolve too.

"Mom!" Laura screamed, panic suffusing her body in a way

even the feeling of a fetus slipping between her legs had not done to her.

Laura watched her mother stumble and fall to her knees on the grass before her. She reached for her daughter, unable to take hold of her. Laura scrambled for purchase against the rocks but couldn't use her muscles to grip.

"Mami, get out!" her mother yelled. It was the first time Laura had been named *mother*, but her body was brown silt rushing away in the current of the creek and she no longer recognized her mother's voice.

HOLDING SPACE

"Take my pain for a while," she begs. Sweat pearls in the dark hair of her arms, above her lip, across her forehead. It's the first time that I have heard her so desperate that she would give it away to me, that she would ask to share tears. Doctors discourage people from sharing tears. They say that tears are toxins leaving the body. How could you be sure what you were taking into your own body?

I wipe her tears away with my fingertips and bring them to my tongue. Agony rushes through me, her aching settles in the tendons above my knees, in the creases of my wide hips, through my wrists like I'm wearing a weighted skin.

"Make it yours," she whispers through her teeth. I have taken her place on the damp bed sheets, no longer able to stand. She gets to her knees and hovers over me, sweeping a brown curl from my forehead. I cover my face as the nerves in my head ignite under my skin.

She straps my legs and feet to our bed as I have done for her so many times before. I have cultivated many ways to comfort her before, but only time and rest could relieve her. My body shakes and radiates, bowing my back off the bed until I am suspended, hovering in space. The pain crescendos along my nerves until I no longer understand what pain is.

"Hold my pain inside you," she says and smiles, "like a handful of keys with no doors, a necklace of nettles, hold it until it belongs to you." She swallows my shout with her lips. This is a nightmare she has survived before. Lying next to me, her kiss is no longer feverish. "Pobrecita," she calls me. Her hand settles over my straining wild heart. "You can hold the aching orb of my life inside of you. It will always be mine."

THIS NIGHT WORLD

Turn the volume up.

No matter that it was her third year of recording in the dark, crouching below oak and pecan trees lifting her shotgun microphone higher; every time Talia heard the telltale hooting of the male Great Horned Owl and the answering screech of the female, sometimes closer, sometimes farther away, her skin prickled. Adjusting her headphones only brought the ambient noises of the night closer to her conscious mind, like the world was pressing close around her, breathing against her skin.

Talia swept her dark curtain of bangs out of her eyes and adjusted the huge, padded headphones on her ears. They rubbed against the other side of her head whose shaved fuzz was slowly growing back over the winding black vine tattoo snaking up her neck and behind her ear. She'd been kneeling in the scrub brush for over an hour. The cold creeped into the joints of her hands, her knees, her ankles. She wasn't as young as she used to be when she first started this work, but there was still something thrilling about preserving the haunting call and response of the owls to listen back to and share with the ornithologists she worked with, as well as uploading to the conservation database that was shared with local university biology students all the way to elementary kids.

The Avian Research and Conservation Institute had her out doing field work near a central Texas wildlife preserve that was surrounded by new housing developments encroaching into the hills. Construction noises and children playing sometimes polluted the recordings, but once deeper into the trees, Talia could hear more clearly the hooting in the waning light. She'd been out there almost every night for three weeks, patiently cataloguing the calls for the small population of owls nesting in that preserve. More than one owl had died swooping in front of cars on the highway or were displaced from their roosting spots because of the construction. It was nice to hear the calls of those who remained.

Tonight, Talia had recorded a few good calls, including the screech of a female roosting nearby and the duets of a male and female, one pitching high and the other answering in a lower hoot, the call and response moving from tree to tree, sometimes closer and sometimes farther away from her in the darkness. In the twilight, Talia saw the black outlines of two owls sitting patiently on the same tree, one on the upper branch, the other below, calling into the night. She hoped she would hear a female call that was almost always shriller and more piercing than the others. The last three nights she'd been sitting out here in the damp brush after a chill November rain. This particular call came without warning. It wasn't responding to a male's hooting in the dark but seemed to come through her headphones like a lost call all on its own. In fact, Talia noticed that every time she heard this female, the male calls in the vicinity fell silent.

The high-pitched series of hoots finally came far off to her left, and Talia walked in an awkward crouch around the bases of trees to get a little closer to this noise. One colleague used to say that when you heard the right bird call through the headphones, it shimmered. Talia hoped to capture some of that magic tonight.

Talia's grandmother used to tell her and her brothers the stories of the Lechuza, the owl witch woman who would carry off kids who misbehaved, not listening to their elders. At her house in McAllen that ran up against a creek, Grandma would tuck Talia into the twin bed with her younger brother Jorge. When they heard the tell-tale sound of what Talia now knew was a barred owl calling from the tree outside their window in that all-too-familiar *who cooks for you, who cooks for us all*, Grandma would pull the covers up to their chins, reminding them "Go to sleep, the Lechuza snatches little kids who don't go to bed on time." To hear Abuela tell it, if someone was bad enough, the Lechuza could take their very soul.

Her abuela knew a man who wandered around after getting drunk at the bar. He had wandering eyes, wandering hands, and would come home drunk, swaying and screaming at his wife and his children. Sometimes he did more than scream. Walking back to his house one night, he heard the owl calling him and, in a fit of drunken rage, began throwing rocks into the trees, searching for the owl whose call tormented him. When his eyes finally met the Lechuza's, she swooped down and snatched his eyes right out of his head. From then on, he never drank another drop and his only wandering around town was to tell anyone who would listen about the witch owl who took his eyes.

Jorge would cuddle into Talia's side and hide his head under the covers once their grandma went to bed, cocooning into the safe warmth of her armpit. But Talia would turn her face to the window, listening for the haunting call of the owl and watching for the iridescent glow of its eyes.

Now, when Talia sought out the owls, she thought of the Lechuza stories as warnings from her grandmother about what a woman-turned-monster could become. She asked her grandma once where the Lechuza came from, and if she was a witch or an owl.

"She is both, and neither. Lechuzas are what happens when a woman turns from God, from her duties as wife and mother, to a different life of evil and darkness."

Later, Talia read a recorded legend from Mexico that said the Lechuza was a woman who shapeshifted into an owl and became a vengeful spirit taking revenge on those who wronged her in life. Her grandmother's emphasis on what a "good woman" was made her wonder if she ever wished she could sprout feathers and fly away from her cruel husband who ignored her and insulted her by turn.

This was same woman who told Talia when she turned twenty-one never to buy sex toys because they would ruin her for her future husband. Talia never found the heart or the courage to tell her she had a girlfriend who had lovingly accompanied her to the sex shop to purchase her very first strap-on. When she thought about it later, Talia felt sorry for her abuela, but she never forgot her stories, if only because they came unbidden to her when she sat listening in the dark.

Call me closer.

There was the call of the lone female owl again, coming from one of the trees to her left. After a few minutes of silence in which no other owl responded, Talia tried to mimic the lower, throatier hooting of the male owls. She stared into the night, willing her human eyes to let in the darkness the way they let in the light. That haunting call came in response and Talia held her mic higher to get a quality recording. She mimicked the male call again, smiling wide when this lone female call came closer than before. They went back and forth like that for a few minutes, call and response, though Talia knew she was compromising the recording with her own voice.

A shadow darker than the night around her swooped over Talia's head, making two arching circles. It was closer to the size of a sandhill crane than an owl. The creature landed silently in front of Talia. It appeared as an owl with piercing yellow eyes until it wrapped its wings around its body and began to grow. It spread and shifted its tawny wings, revealing the full expanse of a body that matched the brown of her feathers that ran along her outstretched wings. When she lifted her head, the Lechuza stared right into Talia's eyes with her yellow ones, shifting her wide hips and full thighs from side to side as if testing their weight on the soft, damp leaf covered ground, though her feet were not human toes but huge tufted talons. Brown, yellow, and orange feathers covered her wings, chest, and the back of her head, ending in the two horned tufts on either side that Talia ached to touch. Her face was rounded with dark furrowed brows that connected in a V on her forehead and her lips were black as an owl's beak.

The Lechuza hopped and stepped across the ground toward Talia, who dropped her recording equipment and let her headphones dangle around her neck. The creature came within a foot of Talia, quirking its head from side to side and studying her features.

Talia realized that the creature was backing her into a black walnut tree when her back hit bark. She felt pressure building between her thighs, a slickness that made her already damp black jeans rub together. She wondered if the Lechuza could smell her, was mapping out her body with its eyes. When she approached close enough for Talia to feel her hot breath on her face, the creature croaked, "Why did you call me?"

"I, I, I—didn't know I was calling you."

The Lechuza quirked her head again, pressing against Talia's body, covering her with her wings in a tight, warm embrace. Talia's eyes closed and she thrust her neck up toward the lips of the creature, a foolhardy thing to do to a famed predator, but the Lechuza sniffed and nuzzled her there and along her chest. Talia felt both aroused and protected, but she kept her eyes squeezed shut as her abuela's voice flickered in her ear to protect her eyes, and her precious soul.

"You smell…" the Lechuza croaked, nibbling gently behind Talia's ear. She didn't finish the thought, and Talia found she didn't care, lost in the sensation of being appraised by the creature.

"Do you want to go with me?" the Lechuza rasped. "Do you want to be mine?"

With eyes still pressed tight, Talia stammered a "Yes," into the cocoon of air between them.

The Lechuza ran her right wing down Talia's back like she was unzipping her. In the wake of this touch, Talia felt her nerve endings burst with a fiery, prickling sensation where feathers sprouted across the surface of her skin like she was a bag being turned inside out. The pleasure-pain swept through her body, making Talia scream. The Lechuza kept her cocooned, watching the transformation intently. Talia's arms flapped out around her and her back and arms were now covered in feathers as dark as her hair. Blood burst from her mouth where her teeth pushed themselves out by the roots and hair fell from her head in soft clumps. Talia's features smoothed, extending, forming her mouth to a sharp brown point though she continued to croak and cry. Her tennis shoes burst at the toes where bright brown talons now steadied her, and Talia tested their balance, screeching into the night in her new owl voice.

The Lechuza hopped back on her talons and studied this new owl woman whose name didn't really matter anymore. She spread her wings up and wide, crouched so her new mate would know how to take flight. Their wing beats were slow, measured movements that gusted wind around them in soundless waves. Finally, they took flight and give chase into the wild darkness.

***

The director of the Avian Research and Conservation Institute found the abandoned recording equipment Talia had checked out days later in the preserve cushioned by a tuft of soft downy feathers. Playing back the recordings, she heard a long duet between two female owls, call and response, fading in and out of range before taking flight to parts unknown.

A FUTURE YOU
NEVER ASKED FOR

The cryosleep chamber hisses open, pressure releasing into the air around Ita's head.

A hand extends to help her climb out of the chamber. There is a tall white woman with her silver-blonde hair slicked back in a net holding a towel toward her, presumably to wipe down her face. She wears a blue medical mask and says, "Welcome back."

Her psychiatrist made it clear: it was this experimental treatment or involuntary hospitalization. When she went in, the doctors told her that all she would do was dream, suspended in time. Her pain would be paused, as would her hunger and other physical needs. It was easier this way to stop people in pain from taking their own lives. "If you give us this time," she told Ita during the counseling session that was required prior to signing off on the treatment, "we may have a better treatment for your pain by the time you wake up."

Ita uses the towel to wipe her face, which is surprisingly moist. She takes several deep breaths and then tests the reflexes of her toes, twists her ankles, bends her knees. Her muscles tingle and feel weak like first waking after a deep sleep, but not ten years' worth of atrophy. She swings her legs over the side of the chamber and tests them against the ground. They are firm, but have gone more pale without sun exposure. She begins to stand, allowing the circulation to rush through her tight hips and down her legs.

"You're moving well! The chamber exercises your muscles while you are in cryosleep to prevent atrophy. Would you like some water?" The nurse holds out a cold bottle of water to Ita. It is sweating and feels incredible against her hand.

"We haven't eliminated plastic bottles in the last ten years?"

The woman smiles under the mask, her eyes crinkling, like she's been through this ten times today.

"There is a new company that makes bottles out of a fiber that is completely biodegradable. So no need to worry."

Ita drinks the water down greedily and smacks her lips into a smile.

"When you are ready, we will help you get dressed, and then take you to the re-entry room for reorientation." This woman, who Ita can now see has a name tag that reads Judith, hands her a white robe. Ita remembers that she is completely naked.

She runs her hands down her arms, over her chest, which has thinned, and behind her neck, searching out the surgery scar where they first tried to treat her. Some things haven't faded. Her fingertips slide along the raised shiny length of it winding up to the base of her skull. On her chest over her heart there is a port she remembers them implanting in her before she went under to best deliver medications into her blood stream.

As they walk by another one of the cryo chamber rooms, Ita is startled by the hurried voices of others dressed like Judith rushing around a half-open chamber. Pulpy red blood seeps through the seams of the chamber onto the floor. Ita thinks that one of the attendants might step in it and fall. There is a faint scream, then Judith ushers Ita along the corridor.

Judith leads Ita away quickly into another room down the hall. This room is an examination room with an exam table in the middle and a desk against the wall crowded with instruments. Judith pulls opens a small tablet screen wrapped around her wrist and begins inputting data. She takes Ita's temperature, looks at her eyes, ears and throat, takes her blood pressure twice over the course of ten minutes and records her findings in her tablet.

"You'd think that after ten years, they would have gotten rid of the sterile paper that crackles under your ass on these exam tables," Ita muses aloud. Again, Judith's cheeks move under the mask in a grimace or a smile.

"Your vital signs all seem normal. We will monitor you for a little while longer while you are at the facility before sending you home. Then, you have an appointment with your physician scheduled for later this week."

"What day is today?"

"It's Tuesday."

Ita has forgotten what a Tuesday even feels like.

Judith takes Ita into the reorientation room. It is a small round room with only one door and concrete seats against one wall. It reminds her of a stadium where her father once took her to watch a sea lion show. On the other wall a large television screen is installed with the words "Welcome" stamped across it in blue letters. She stares at it, watching the words translate to different languages.

"During this reorientation video, we will give you a sense of some big changes that have taken place over the last five years in the world at large and in your community. We find that this has been helpful to provide a sense of stable reality."

Ita blinks for a moment and looks down.

"I was supposed to be under for ten years. What do you mean?"

For the first time, Judith appears off kilter. She types into her tablet and scrolls through what Ita assumes is her file.

"It says that your contract term was changed by your family since you made them your medical power of attorney. They may have changed the length of your stay."

Ita stares down at the smooth concrete floor, so smooth it reflects her face in gray.

"Is my family here?"

Judith smiles again under the mask, complacent, and nods.

"We find it best to go through this process first before reintroducing you to your loved ones. The first reunion can be…overwhelming."

Judith touches her tablet and the room darkens as the video on the screen begins to play soothing music. A calm voice starts by describing the year and some of the major events Ita has missed.

We are excited to welcome you back to the world in 2026. We hope that your time away will provide a new perspective and that you are excited for the new treatment opportunities that await you.

On screen, Ita watches a clip show overlaid with soothing instrumental music. A blonde, white woman she doesn't recognize is elected president to much fanfare and political abuse. Wildfires across the west coast rage, flooding in the Gulf, headlines about the climate crisis and a new spiked pathogen loom across the screen, but also an emphasis on hopeful things, carbon offsets, restoration of small portions of the rainforest, coral reefs that had undergone bleaching slowly restoring themselves, a peace accord between several nations previously at war, new labor contracts for artists and writers in Hollywood, and free college tuition for all in the United States.

The screen fades to black and the lights come back on. Ita sits still on the stone bench with her head down, breathing.

"What's next?"

Judith takes her to the next room where Ita changes into new clothes and shoes that are comfortable cotton in drab colors. She notices how her skin hangs on her frame, the muscle tone and weight she has lost around her hips and stomach, which were always full and round.

Each new room feels like they are following the path of a museum exhibit. As they move through the reorientation process, it occurs to Ita that as her body has come more alive from the cryosleep state, she had not yet felt any pain.

Judith hands Ita a mask.

"Until your doctor clears you, you will need to wear this protective mask at all times when you are outdoors and in the company of others. You are not accustomed to how the air quality may have changed, and there are new allergens and pathogens that your immune system will not be able to fight until you can receive your new immunizations. The doctor will go over all of this on Friday."

Ita puts the blue surgical mask over her face and waits for the door at the other side of the room to open. When it does, her parents slowly step through wearing masks of their own, tears welling in their eyes. The most striking change is that Ita's father's thick, normally dark eyebrows have gone entirely gray against his brown skin. Her mother has lost weight and looks so small Ita is afraid that hugging her might break her.

Then, Ita's partner Dean walks in behind them. Her parents hug her and she stares over their shoulders at Dean with tears in her eyes.

Before she went to sleep, she had told him it was over, that he should treat her as if she had died and live his life without the hope of her returning. They both knew the risks when she signed up for this procedure. Neither could know for sure that Ita would wake up, that her organs wouldn't fail, that she wouldn't suffer damage to her brain and lose all memory of him.

Dean moves closer to the group and Ita's parents make room for him.

Ita hates how the wrinkles around the corners of his bright gray eyes make her want to kiss him. She hates that he waited for this reunion with her.

Dean steps up and cups a hand behind her head, drawing her closer and leaning his forehead against her own since they can't kiss yet.

"Hi baby," he says, his normally deep voice waterlogged. Ita doesn't resist, maybe because she wants this, maybe because her muscles are too weak from cryostasis to pull away. She leans her weight against him, feeling solid for the first time since she's woken up. Hot tears burn in the corners of her eyes and she pulls back to look at him, and her parents.

"What happened? Why did y'all wake me up before my term ended?"

Her parents look down, then past her to Dean as he takes her hand in his.

"It was too much, baby. Too long to be without you, and your doctor called your parents to tell them that the FDA approved a new treatment program that she thinks will work for you!"

His eyes are so hopeful, light dawning over a cool gray winter morning. He hugs one side of her while her parents flank her other side and they approach Judith to finish the discharge procedures before they take her home. Ita had always loved their closeness before; now their need to have hands on her at all times makes her feel like she is melting.

In the car, Dean drives and her parents sit in the back seat with her, suffocating her with their loving weight. Her mother holds her hand in a cold, bony but incredibly strong grip. Every time Ita looks over at her, her mother's cheeks lift behind the mask and she whispers, "My baby, mi chula is back," and runs her thumb over the skin of her hand. Ita gets used to sensation again, to her nerve endings reacting to stimuli, to touch.

"Are you hungry amor? How do you feel?" her father asks. "Your mom made a lot of food."

"Miguel, remember the nurse said she can't dive right back into eating solid food right away. They gave us supplement drinks that she needs to drink for a few days before then," Dean tells her father, patting the cardboard box in the passenger's seat. Ita's skin prickles every time he called her father by his first name.

"That's okay, Pa. I'll come over to eat another day," Ita reassures him.

Instead of getting on the highway to go south to her parent's house, Dean drives north from the cryogenics center to the house they had been renting for a year before Ita made the decision to go under. After twenty minutes, Dean pulls up to their driveway. The little house painted sky blue looks exactly as she remembers it, though Dean has let the oak tree's branches cast too much shadow over the roof and the bushes around the side of the house need trimming.

Inside, the brightness from the natural light of their home has dimmed. It looks like a layer of dust has settled over all the surfaces, like a museum of their lives together that Dean kept untouched for this moment. It doesn't feel real. Ita runs her hand along the books on the shelves, the ugly thrifted yellow lamp Dean loves, the blue ceramic vase her parents got them when they moved in together sitting on the small round kitchen table just to ground herself that she is here as nostalgic memory and present slam into her. She grips the table and her father comes up behind her.

"I know mi'ja, just take it easy. Go slowly. It's going to take some time." He didn't know though, he would never know. Ita had traveled through time and come out into a world that was just as heavy as the world she left.

Dean puts the box of supplement drinks in the kitchen and pulls out the chair so Ita can sit. He gives her a bottle of water, which they watch her drink in silence.

"Where is Misha?" Ita asks, looking around for their brown and black speckled tabby, who was usually on the ottoman at this time of day. Dean looks down sadly.

"Mish passed two years ago babe. He had kidney disease."

Ita nods, rubs her hands up and down her legs, her go-to grounding exercise. She doesn't know what she expected when she woke up. She was supposed to have ten years, and maybe a part of her agreed to this long sleep because she didn't believe she would ever wake up, that the cryosleep would take care of the problem for her. This was like kicking the can way down the road, except she has no ownership over what has happened since she signed her name on the release forms.

Her mother rubs her hand up and down Ita's back. The familiar feeling flashes through and the tears start again.

"What else? Might as well give me the updates," Ita laughs. Her parents look to Dean, who is leaning against the kitchen counter with his arms crossed across his chest. She imagines the conversations they've had before she woke up, the preparations they've made to be cautiously hopeful, tamping down their own fierce need to touch her and make sure that she is really here.

"The doctor doesn't want us to overwhelm you. We can share as we go, but I think you should take it easy," Dean tells her. It still surprises her how much her parents defer to her partner, even now.

They liked him well enough when she and Dean first got together, always welcomed him into their home, but now they follow his lead like he is her husband, like they've decided they are still together. No one has asked her that yet.

"Ok, I guess. I need to go to the bathroom."

Everyone stands when she does and watches her retreat to the bathroom down the hall. Ita locks the door. In the mirror flecked with toothpaste, she stares at her mushed, stale auburn curls falling almost to her back. She takes off her mask and splashes water across her sallow face. Her eyes are sunken and bruised. On the black wire shelf next to the sink, Ita sees Dean's electric shaver. She flips it on and takes it to the right side of her head, letting her crumpled tendrils of hair fall to the white tiles beneath her bare feet. She leaves behind a soft fuzz and snips the curls on her left side to her chin, taking lost years off her face. She looks more alive now. Rummaging through the rest of Dean's things on his shelf, she finds a small packet of condoms. They had stopped using condoms after they moved in together, but then again, they had stopped having sex after her second hospitalization. A flutter of innate possessiveness runs through her chest, followed by a deep well of sadness that despite his best efforts, he hadn't found anyone else to love more than the hope of Ita. She hopes that at least he fucked a few people while she was asleep. She hopes that he enjoyed it.

Her parents leave reluctantly when Ita returns with her hair shorn off. Clearly, they decide, she is overwhelmed. They promise to return to see her in the morning. Dean instructs Ita to drink one of the supplement drinks when the hunger hits her. It tastes like berry flavored chalk, like Flintstones vitamins dumped in a blender. Dean leads her to their bedroom where the sheets have been cleaned and he has lit a candle to make the room smell less musty.

"We can't sleep in the same room until you get your vaccinations on Friday, so I'm going to sleep on the guest bed in the office."

"I can sleep in there, you don't have to give me the bedroom," Ita says, stripping off her shirt without thinking. She isn't wearing a bra, and Dean just watches her bare body move before him, a first sighting in five years.

"It's fine, I don't mind. I made sure everything was clean in here, and I have a HEPA filter running so you can take off your mask when you sleep." He continues to watch her as she pulls on a fresh clean tank top and new pajama shorts he had laid out on the bed. "You've lost weight."

Ita runs her hands over her arms and chest. They are bonier.

"Yeah, some of my bulk is gone. Can't weight lift in my dreams," she laughs.

"Hopefully in a few days we can get you eating solid food again. Here's some water." Dean hands her a glass. Before she moves away, he pulls her in, resting his forehead against hers. Through their masks, the condensation of his breath moistens the blue paper like his breath longs to mingle with hers. Ita wonders what his lips would taste like. Then he pulls away, saying goodnight and retreating down the hall before Ita closes the door on his footsteps.

She takes off her mask to drain the glass of water and sits on the side of the bed. There is so much she would rather do than be inert again, to sleep again, so she paces instead, doing lunges across the bedroom carpet, concentrating on the soft burn of the fibers beneath her sensitive feet, the creak of her unused knees, seeing how many jumping jacks she can do in a body she both recognizes and doesn't. No sleep comes, only her restless feet against the carpet all night.

Dean insists on driving her to the appointment on Friday with Dr. Leage. In the car, he plays a song she doesn't recognize. He sings aloud, laughing at how silly he looks. It is both familiar to her and makes her itchy with annoyance, like expecting the crisp bite of an apple and finding it watery instead.

She doesn't know why she expected the traffic to be better on the way there, or that everyone would have electric cars and adequate shelter. There are still as many encampments of houseless folks under the highway, still as many cars on the road, if not more, and more smog in the air than she remembers. Maybe it was too much to expect in five short years.

Ita stretches and rolls her neck. The pain had been creeping back in the last two days, a hazy sensation that she both knew as though no time had passed, but still felt surprised to find in her body. The more it has grown up her head and down her spine, the more she hates how her body expected this all along.

Dr. Leage's office is on the fifth floor of an office park with black-tinted windows. It looks both ordinary and nefarious. In the waiting room, everyone is required to wear a mask since this is a specialty clinic only treating those suffering with chronic pain and other chronic conditions, some of whom went through the same clinical trials, the same cryosleep Ita did. Some people wear theirs below their noses and Dean seats them farther away, holding Ita's hand as though she is a scared child going to the doctor for the first time. Ita fills out the same paperwork she has filled out a thousand times before, though it has been five years, and this time on a tablet with streaks of fingerprints across the surface of the screen.

When a nurse in light-blue scrubs with golden stars calls Ita's name, Dean asks her if she wants him to go back with her. Technically, she gave him permission to have access to her medical records in the past. This time she doesn't list his name, or her parents.

"I'm good. I'll show you the doctor's notes when I'm done." Her hand trails across his shoulders. She follows the nurse through the door and down the familiar hallway to Room 5, the room they always put her in. She is instructed to remove her clothes and don a medical gown and grippy socks. Ita rips open the package. These are a soft pink, a color she doesn't have, and feels a little thrill putting them on and knowing they will join her other pile in the drawer at home.

Dr. Leage comes in, wide smile under her blue mask, taking Ita's hands in her freezing cold ones and squeezing them hard, genuinely happy to see her. There are more white hairs mixed into the black around the temples, and crows' feet along her eyes, but otherwise time collapses, and Ita is back where she has always been, sitting on the crinkling sterile paper and waiting for her body to be assessed.

"Lupita, it's so good to see you. I am sure things have been overwhelming the last few days since you woke up, but I have really been looking forward to this appointment. You're only my third patient to undergo the cryostasis treatment and one of them is still under. I'm so glad you're here with us today." Dr. Leage's voice has always been genuine and warm, her golden eyes really taking Ita in behind the black-rimmed glasses.

"It's been okay. A little weird for sure, but good I guess," she says, wondering if she should correct the doctor once again about her name. They are still holding hands.

"How have you been feeling since you woke up?"

Ita shrugs. "There's been some pain, especially around my neck and the base of my skull." She rubs it now, remembering how she had shorn off the hair there to a light fuzz.

"Mmmhm, that's to be expected. You're aware of your nerves again and naturally the pain is going to come back to you."

Like an old friend, Ita thinks.

"Let me do a quick assessment and see where we are," the doctor says. She lets go of Ita's hands and pulls on some new gloves. They aren't the typical blue silicone gloves Ita is used to seeing, but thicker white gloves with mesh padding. Once they are on, the palms of the gloves turn blue.

"I'm going to start my exam now. If the gloves sense your nerves firing off more than usual, they'll tell me."

Dr. Leage passes her gloved hands over Ita's face, the sides of her head, her neck and down her shoulders like a ghost's touch. Around her neck and shoulders, the gloves light turns from blue, its neutral setting, to a yellow and then to a bright, pulsing red like a metal detector finding buried treasure on a beach. Once she finishes moving her hands across all of Ita's extremities, she pushes a button on the side of the glove. Ita can see data flashing across the computer screen resting on a rolling table where the doctors and nurses take notes. The doctor sits back down on her rolling stool to review the data.

"Your blood circulation, heart rate, lung function, and kidney function look good. I'm not detecting any blood clots anywhere as you might expect to find after such a long time being immobile, which tells me they really know what they're doing over there at the lab! The areas where the glove lit up, around your brain stem and vagus nerve, indicate lingering neuropathic pain, the kind we were treating since the car accident. In some ways, that is encouraging! I don't detect any new issues, just the same ones you were dealing with, and those may improve on their own with time. So I'm not recommending we start you on any new medications until we schedule you for your first pain reprocessing therapy session next week."

Ita swings her feet back and forth where they hang off the examination table and opens her hands for the doctor to continue.

"This is the therapy that I have been talking to your partner and parents about. When it became available, I was so excited I called Dean right away! This treatment allows us to use specialized psilocybin derived from a variety of mycelia and a synthetic protein to provide a controlled therapeutic experience to reprogram your nervous system so that your pain is reduced, possibly even cured indefinitely!"

"Like magic mushrooms?"

Dr. Leage looks knowingly into Ita's eyes.

"They aren't magic, but they are damn effective! The clinic has had several successful trials with treating folks with Complex PTSD and other chronic pain disorders like fibromyalgia, and you are the perfect candidate!"

"Sounds exciting."

Dr. Leage takes Ita's hands in hers again.

"I know you must be feeling very overwhelmed right now. But I want you to know, a life free from the pain cycle you have been living with is possible, and I am going to do my best to make sure your treatment is successful. Until next week, I want you to continue drinking those meal supplement drinks and plenty of water, and write down any time you are experiencing pain, like a log. Don't just say you are in pain, but describe the severity, the feelings of it, is it sharp, stabbing, pulsing, etc. This will help you prepare for the therapy next week."

The doctor hands her a little blue journal with a rainbow framed by two clouds embossed across the cover. Ita takes it and tucks it into her tote bag.

"Now, let's get your vaccinations done. These are going to leave you feeling pretty fatigued, maybe even a little feverish. They should cover you for the three most common viruses circulating right now since the outbreak we had four years ago. I'm sure you're glad you got to skip past that!" Dr. Leage puts on her blue silicone gloves and rolls over a tray holding four needles, rolling up Ita's shirt sleeves and giving her two in each arm, the syringes plunging deep into her muscle like a cold punch.

"I'm sending Dean home with some additional instructions. You can take Tylenol for soreness or if you spike a fever, and in two days or so, you should be able to be around other people and start eating soft solid foods again. Just nothing too spicy!" She places pink band-aids across the puncture wounds on Ita's arms and chuckles. Ita laughs internally, thinking of the chile-to-tomato ratio her mom usually uses to make any salsa, even the mild ones. Good luck with that.

It's still a few days before Dean can kiss Ita, according to Dr. Leage. The updated vaccines create faster immune responses and are more sterilizing to prevent infections since the beginning of the Sars-Covid 19 pandemic. Dean shared news articles with her and she'd read about how fast it spread, how it took so many lives, including one of her aunts and her cousin, people she hoped she would never have to miss. Dean didn't say who he lost.

One morning, Ita comes out of their bedroom, having slept on the floor for a few hours after her nighttime exercises, and Dean is standing at the stove spooning oatmeal into a bowl sans mask.

"Hey baby, you're cleared to eat solids today! I thought you might like to try these organic oats I got from that mill downtown."

Dean hands her the bowl, pulls her into his side and rubs his lightly stubbled cheek against hers, fuzz meeting fuzz. She is asked to surrender something, and she doesn't yet know what. Dean's dry lips skate across her cheek at the corner of her mouth where he breathes her in. There was a time she craved this closeness, this fusion. Ita relishes his warmth like the kiss is happening in a dream full of pinks and oranges and her body is floating in a space having skipped past his longing, which presses against her through the glass wall of his heart.

He releases her to eat. The oatmeal is perfect, rich and nutty with flax meal and cinnamon sprinkled on top. The first mouthful burns deliciously. Once she is done devouring the bowl, Dean washes it clean and leaves it on the dryer rack. So much care, Ita thinks, from someone she doesn't deserve. She approaches him at the counter, pressing against his solid back until he turns in her arms, hugging and kissing her, turning her so that her back is against the counter and drops to his knees, mouthing at her belly and hips beneath her sleep shorts. She lets him pull them down and get his mouth on her, opening to him with a deep breath because she wants this but he wants it more. His lips and tongue are both patient and frantic, and when she comes, bracing against his pliant face, he pulls away and begins to cry. Ita watches him at her feet. She rakes her hand through his impossibly soft hair, feeling the deep prickle of shame and satisfaction at taking this pleasure from him. Ita brings him to her lips.

"Thank you baby. What's going on?"

Dean sniffs, wipes his mouth and eyes with the back of his hand.

"I wasn't sure I was ever going to have this again. With you."

"I know."

An apology lingers on her lips, but what would that "I'm sorry" do to soothe the open wound between them? Apologies meant nothing to people who weren't supposed to be alive.

Now that Ita is cleared for more contact, they go to dinner at her parent's house where her mother makes green chile enchiladas filled with chicken and rice and beans. She loads Ita's paper plate until it starts to bend under the weight while rubbing her hand across Ita's scar, an old habit she'd forgotten her mother did since the accident.

"Thank you for cooking, Mom," she says, leaning into that gently prying hand.

"I'm glad you like them," her mother says while she watches Ita eat. She cleans her plate.

They sit in her parents backyard under new twinkle lights, laughing, drinking beer and ciders. Ita's father talks about all the repairs he's done to the house, and her mother shows her her new flower beds and how her herb garden survived the last bad freeze they had. Time is collapsing again. Ita finishes her second helping of enchiladas, knowing her stomach won't thank her later but still stuffing herself with their rich burn.

In her notebook that night, Ita does an exercise a former therapist had given her a long time ago to work against the feelings of isolation she said she was feeling as her pain grew worse over time, before her first hospitalization. Each person she writes is supposed to be part of her support system, the people she can go to when she is struggling. Ita writes her name in the middle of the page and draws a circle around it.

Ita

Around her name, she writes Dean's name, her parents', Dr. Leage, then stops. Many of her friends moved, and many others stopped hanging out with her or even talking with her after her pain became more limiting, after she tried, twice, to leave the earth for good. Once she knew she was going to undergo cryosleep, Ita accepted the loss of her relationships with others. She'd lost so many before. Illness did that. Trying to reconnect to living now feels like a beautifully impossible miracle.

Before the first pain reprocessing therapy session, Ita continues to write entries into the little journal, even as she sits in the waiting room of the clinic. Most people around her are on their phones and ignoring the other people around them but she doesn't have a phone anymore, and Dean hasn't suggested buying a new one yet. Ita doesn't have a job yet, or anywhere else to go, so the urgency to have a device feels external. Instead, she writes or doodles like she used to kill time in middle school between classes, drawing hearts, fractals, cubes and vines along the edge of the paper.

When they call Ita back, she is instructed to take off her shirt and change into a short paper gown. Then, the nurse lays her down on a beige reclining chair set in a row of other chairs, some already inhabited by patients who wear headphones, eyes closed. They look incredibly peaceful.

She still has a port on her chest from being in cryostasis. It's only an inch wide, but the nurse told her when she woke up that it was used to administer medications and nutrients to her while she was asleep, and periodically as a form of dialysis to help with blood circulation during the cryosleep process. In the past, when cryogenics was only for people who had died who wanted to be frozen and brought back, the blood was removed from the body altogether to prevent decay. Now, they use her port to administer the psilocybin compound.

Ita lays her head back against the chair while the nurse dressed in burgundy scrubs, face hidden behind her mask, brings a long thin tube with a needle attachment and inserts it into the port. Then, she attaches wireless electrodes to Ita's temples and forehead, pressing the adhesive into her skin and arranging a sterile pillow behind her head.

"Once I start the first dose, you'll lie here for an hour or so and let it take effect. You may feel a little lightheaded, and more relaxed, even euphoric. If you start to feel anxious or agitated, press this call button here," she says and indicates the red button on the side of the chair, "and I will come and suspend the session. These electrodes are taking data on your brainwaves. Let me know if they get too hot. Afterward, you'll be asked to fill out a survey about your experience. Sound good?"

"I guess so."

"Any questions?"

Ita shakes her head. She wouldn't know what to ask. The nurse presses a button that flashes blue on the pump machine on the floor by her chair and liquid runs up the tube into her port. Ita feels the liquid begin to seep into her bloodstream through her port, almost like a saline IV flush. For the first thirty minutes, she puts on the headphones and listens to nondescript music she imagines was composed for meditations retreats. Someone is using a sound bowl. The reverberation moves through Ita's chest. Her pain isn't gone, there isn't an absence of pain, but rather her body feels suspended above pain, almost like her skin isn't making contact with anything but is in contact with everything.

At some point, she opens her eyes. The gentle yellow light of the lamps in the room, much better than the normal sickly strobe of florescent light in most clinics, pulses like a heartbeat, haloed light coming closer to her eyes than it did before. Next to her, someone is now occupying the lounger, a short woman with rich dark skin and two black braids framing her plump face. She adjusts herself, her eyes closed, moving the headphones around her ears like she is bothered by the feeling of them on her skin. She opens her eyes and finds Ita watching her.

"What's up?" she says, like Ita is trying to get her attention.

"No, nothing, just looking around."

"I'm Erika."

"Ita. Nice to meet you."

They both settle back into their respective dream states, closing their eyes, but Ita wonders what Erika is seeing behind her eyelids, what she feels when her skin makes contact with the leather recliner, whether she, like Ita, would like to ask for a quilt to throw over her legs just to feel a different sensation.

After an hour, Ita feels a gentle pressure on her shoulder. The nurse unhooks the tube from Ita's port, peels the warm electrodes from her skin and hands her a paper cup of ice-cold water, which she sips gratefully. Erika is still going through her own session, eyes clenched. Sweat droplets cling to the fine hairs of her upper lip.

"I am going to ask you to answer five questions about your experience on this tablet. This helps us to establish goals for your treatment and learn more about our patients' experiences. Please be as candid as possible and bring it back to the front when you are done."

On the screen, Ita scrolls through the questions:

1. *Please rate your pain or discomfort on a scale from one being almost no pain, to ten being the worst pain you have ever experienced.*

2. *On a scale of one to five, one being very little and five being extreme, how would you rate your sense of peace during or after your session?*

3. *On a scale of one to five, one being very little and five being extreme, how would you rate your feeling of being part of an interconnected whole during or after your session?*

4. *On a scale of one to five, one being very little and five being extreme, how would you rate your feelings of surrender to the infinite during or after your session?*

5. *Please comment with any specific feelings you had before your session today and how these feelings may have changed after your session.*

Ita fills out the questionnaire as best she can, her muscles still relaxed and pliant, her nerves not firing off signals at the same rate they are used to. Her hand slips when she hands the tablet back to the nurse. On the way back to the lobby, Ita pulls her mask back on, glad she doesn't have to school her features once she is outside.

Erika shows up to three of Ita's next four therapy appointments. On the third session, Erika rushes in a few minutes late and sits in the recliner next to Ita again.

"Hey again." Ita waves. Erika gives a weak wave back as she drops her bulky tote bag from a local bookstore printed with an owl perched on a branch and sits down to catch a breath.

"Hey. Sorry, remind me of your name again."

Ita smiles. "It's Ita."

"Right, thanks. Good to see you again. Sorry, I ran here from work."

"No worries. Where do you work?"

Erika's breathing slows as she pats the knees of her strategically ripped black jeans. "I got a part-time job as a bookseller for the Book Nook downtown, just to help out my parents until I finish this therapy regimen, but it's tough when we have to go to these sessions twice a week. I had to cut out of helping with inventory, but my boss has been understanding. She has Lupus so she gets it."

Ita nods, thinking about Dean and her parents supporting her right now and how little attachment she has felt to finding work or establishing a routine again. She still hasn't asked how much of the cryosleep study was covered because it is still experimental and how much they had to pay for.

"I get it."

"Yeah, they gave me a few weeks since I woke up, but I didn't feel right just sitting around. I may have to scale back my hours though."

"You were in the cryosleep program too?" Ita asks, leaning forward. This is the first person she's met who went through the program at the same time she did.

"Yep. I was gone for five years."

"Me too. It was supposed to be ten, but I guess this treatment became available sooner and my partner and parents didn't want to wait." Ita looks down at her feet rubbing across the firm clinic carpet, which is a pristine blue despite the traffic of feet it must see.

"Damn, that sucks. I mean, sorry, it doesn't suck that you are here, I just mean it sucks that they made that decision for you," Erika breathes out all at once. Gratitude sweeps through Ita in a wave she isn't expecting that makes her want to cry. She hasn't cried in so long.

"Thank you. I've been back for a month and no one has acknowledged that."

Erika smiles, laying her hand on Ita's for a moment.

"Happy to say it. I don't always have the best brain-to-mouth filter, especially when I have a fibro flare, but at the end of it all, only we know what this experience has been like."

They disconnect when the nurse Clarissa sweeps in to get them both hooked up and ready for their next dose. As the psilocybin takes effect, Ita imagines Erika at the bookstore, the layout she still recalls from a visit years before. She can imagine that bright smile as Erika helps a customer find a book they are looking for, her excitement at unboxing a new delivery and entering the books into the computer system before stocking the shelves and making a cute "staff picks" display for new releases. She doesn't know why she can picture this so vividly when she barely knows Erika. Maybe she hates this job and watches the clock until her shift is over. But no, her tote bag has fallen over from the weight of new books Erika probably can't wait to take them home and read.

"Ready to go back into dreamland?" Erika asks Ita.

They lie back in the recliners, holding their breaths as the doses enters their bloodstreams. Erika waits until the nurse has left the room before she reaches across her armchair to hook her finger around Ita's hand.

Ita squeezes Erika's hand. She watches the warm yellow lights in the ceiling begin to pulse into halos that radiate through her eyes, into her neck and down her spine until they match Erika's steady heartbeat pulsing in her fingertips.

"Are you getting there?" Ita asks.

"Oh yeah, I'm off."

Holding onto Erika's hand grounds Ita, keeps her from feeling like she is going to fly off the recliner too far into that warm light.

In her chest, the light settles and grows to a burning, white hot pain she has never felt before. Her lungs constrict as stabbing, hot pain shoots into her legs, her feet, all the way into her toes and down her arms. Beside her, Erika arches her back off the recliner in a sharp cry of pain and squeezes Ita's hand tighter. Soon, the intense feeling subsides with several deep breaths, but when Ita looks over at Erika she is sweating, tears tracking down her brown cheeks and wetting her surgical mask.

"That was something new. I thought this shit was supposed to calm our nervous systems so that we would experience fewer pains, not all new ones," Erika says, sitting up in her seat.

"What did you feel?"

Erika blinks back at Ita. Her eyelashes kiss her cheeks.

"A sharp pain from my head to my neck and down my shoulder. Then it started to pulse and move like a bead of white-hot light across my nerves." Ita recognizes this feeling, though she's never heard it described this way.

"I felt like lightning was striking my whole body."

"That sounds like my fibromyalgia, when it gets really bad."

"Are you saying I can literally feel your pain?" Ita asks.

"What?! No. How would that happen?"

Ita runs her hand over her port with one hand, still holding Erika's hand.

"I don't know. Maybe we're so sensitive that we're becoming psychically linked," Ita posits. Their hands sway between them. The sudden shock of pain is fading, but Ita's nerves feel alight with new sensitivity.

When their sessions end and they've answered their post-therapy questionnaires, Ita asks Erika for her phone number. It is the only number besides Dean's and her parents' home phone that she has. Her circle of care widens.

In bed, Dean asks Ita if she dreamed when she was in cryosleep.

"Our consciousness was limited. We were sedated into a state where I don't know if our brains could even send the messages of dreams into our minds. Sometimes I think you need to live to dream." They were facing each other in their bed now that they could sleep together again. He brushes his hand through the fuzz of her hair, seeming to relish the new sensation.

"I guess that makes me sad. That whole time, you had nothing to console you, or pass the time," he whispers.

"Why are you whispering?"

"I don't know," he says, smiling.

"Think of it like putting a pause on existing."

That's how Ita thinks of it. But if she's being honest, after the first therapy treatment, dreams from that unconscious time are coming back to her. At times, she did dream of familiar people like Dean, or a random coworker from years before like her brain was scrolling through the memory rolodex for anything to latch onto. Other dreams had her flying, soaring over lakes and arctic tundras she had only seen in pictures or on TV. The one that comes back to her now is tangible. She's sitting on a beach alone, her feet digging into the heat of the soft sand. As the sun sets on the horizon, a solar flare washes over her in golden waves, one after the other, the waves carry her body into the sky floating on their warm undulating light and Ita is unafraid.

"I read once that mushrooms, well all fungi really, create a network called mycelium that communicate messages to aid in their survival. This network extends to the root systems of other plants and even bacteria. They all help one another to live. Maybe the therapy is changing our brains, like creating new neuropathways that allow us to communicate outside of our bodies." Erika has been explaining this theory for the last fifteen minutes of their session.

"Dude, you're high."

They both erupt into fits of giggles, but Ita keeps a firm hold on Erika's hand. There has to be something to this idea. Their connection and ability to share sensations, to share their pain has only increased over the last few sessions together.

"Has work been any better?" Ita asks. Erika shrugs. She lifts her free hand in front of her face, twiddling her fingers like she is touching the water vapor in the air.

"A little. I feel like the pain has become more manageable. It's integrating back into a life I left that feels so weird."

"Tell me about it."

Ita hasn't looked for a job or thought about what she wants to do after these sessions are over. Sometimes she hopes she won't get better so that she and Erika can keep seeing each other, wondering if Erika will become like all of the other people in her life who grew tired of her pain. Of course, Erika is the first friend she has ever known whose pain consumes her life.

Ita holds tight to Erika and closes her eyes as the wave of lightness takes her again. Before, her mind has often been blissfully blank, but bright color seeps in. An image to latch onto. Erika sitting on a patio outside sipping hot milky chai from a porcelain teacup next to a man who looks like he could be her father, the same sleek black hair and round nose. Erika smiles at the wind whistling through the trees, at her father in his worn sandals, at the world contained in their small, green backyard.

The nurse they normally see walks through their linked hands, breaking their grip, to unhook their ports.

"You both should be concentrating on your own treatments when you're here," she scolds. Erika adjusts her shirt over her port, rolling her eyes in an exaggerated rotation at the nurse's back.

"Did you feel anything different today?" Ita asks her casually after the nurse has removed the electrodes and the lines from their ports.

Erika smiles a secret smile.

"Just that you really like hammocks," she says. Ita guffaws, rubbing her neck self-consciously. She does love hammocks, but what dream had she transmitted that had Erika smiling like that?

Before they leave, the secretary who normally schedules her appointments hands Ita a sealed envelope to take home and review with Dean.

Dean is late to pick her up so Erika offers to drive her home. They live close to the bookshop and Erika has a shift, though she's still giggly from the session. When she gets home, Dean rushes out to the car barefoot, his urgency immediately making Ita's loose body tense.

"Is everything okay? I was about to leave to come get you!"

"Erika, this is my partner Dean. Dean, this is my friend Erika."

Dean stoops low and leans through the window to shake Erika's hand. Up close, Ita surveys the fine brown hairs and freckles on his arm and has an urge to bite down on the muscley flesh.

"Nice to meet you, Dean. It was no problem taking Ita home. I gotta run, but I'll see you next time!" Erika says, her mask crinkling around her round cheeks.

When they get inside, Dean rubs his hands vigorously up and down her arms like he can will her back into existence. He has some rich butternut squash pasta on the stove, and Ita is tempted to go over and steal a spoonful from the pan.

"You know that I'm going to be around other people again right? I have to be allowed to make a life again," she tells him.

"I know that. I just want you to ease back into it. You're still building immunity to stuff and getting used to being back in the world."

Ita takes out the sealed envelope that she was given at the clinic.

"They said we should review this together."

Dean takes the envelope. On the stove, the sauce is bubbling over. It may be too late to save it before dinner.

He opens the envelope and begins to read, stops, then folds the packet back up again.

"Let's eat first, then we can talk about it later. How was your session today?"

Something breaks in Ita. Dean has always been caring, even tempered their entire relationship. Now it feels forced, like he is trying not to wake a dormant violence in her.

"I think we should talk about it now. What the hell does it say?"

Dean sighs and hands her the packet. She begins to read through some of the language, though it is coded in legalese and doctor speak. Ita discerns that this report covers data collected during her cryosleep and through some of the initial therapy sessions she has completed. At first, the data report is presented for them to review her treatment before she can have her next cat scan and meeting with Dr. Leage, but there is language highlighted at the bottom for Dean to sign, not her.

"What the hell does this mean?"

Dean goes back to the stove to turn off the burner. The sauce is ruined. He sits at their table with his hands clasped. His thumbs swipe across his hand in rhythmic motions.

"We had to pay for this somehow. The clinical trial still came with a lot of costs. They assured us that harvesting your body would only happen if you passed in cryostasis," Dean explains.

"But they did harvest parts of me, isn't that what this says?!" Ita shakes the papers at him.

"They had to take blood and tissue samples anyway to ensure that your body was healthy. What does it matter how those samples were used afterward? You're getting this treatment for free!"

"Setting that aside, this says that the data they are collecting on my brain waves is being harvested too! They are harvesting my mental energy, my fucking dreams?!"

Dean rubs her arms. "Please calm down, it's not as nefarious as you make it sound. They are collecting this data anyway."

What Ita hears is, *"Your pain, your psychic distress, is the ultimate resource to be taken without consent."*

"Does everyone else know they are doing this?! We're only the second group to undergo this treatment."

Dean brushes his hand over her port.

"I wish you could accept that sometimes a good thing can be just that, a good thing."

Ita smacks his hand away.

"I have no control over what I consider a good thing. That seems to be up to everyone else *but* me."

Dean steps back and watches Ita fume, shaking his head.

"You don't know. You just don't know."

"What don't I know?"

"When you signed up for this treatment, I had to see it as hopeful, as something that could lead to a better life for you, but all I knew was that my partner, the person I loved and cared for the most, would do anything not to continue living this life with me."

It was like being sucked into the ground, this feeling. That was what Ita missed most about cryosleep, that she didn't have to consciously feel, or take anyone else's hurt into herself along with her own.

"I'm sorry. I'm sorry that I couldn't be a person who could stick around for you. That's why I told you to let me go the minute I signed the consent form."

"During the pandemic, I lost a friend, people I worked with, my auntie who helped raise me. My parents aren't around. I had no one to turn to because you were gone. My only consolation was that you didn't have to live with that fear," Dean told her.

Ita wonders if her new powers of empathic perception could extend to Dean, if she could hold his hand and take his pain, his dreams into herself like she had Erika's. Even if it is possible, doing that might open an emptiness inside her that nothing could fill.

Ita locks herself into the guest bedroom and doesn't come out until Dean leaves for work the next morning. He had slipped the packet with his signature on it under the door.

Dr. Leage is stern with Ita at her next scan. It warns of aberrations in the data.

"You say your pain isn't as severe, but your nerves are lighting up in places we've never seen before. It's like your nervous system is more activated and not less. And your brain wave data looks really muddled. I'm not getting clear scans. Are you stressed? What's going on?"

Ita runs her hands along her legs, thinking of the sensations she has allowed to light up her nerves every time she touches Erika's hand, a portal of feeling, of dreaming now open between them.

"This is your treatment, Ita. Only you can make it work and keep yourself from being distracted by other people and their issues. I don't want you to come back to me in a year begging me to put you back in cryosleep again," Dr. Leage says, rubbing her hand into Ita's like a threat.

That night, Ita texts Erika her plan. For a few hours, Erika doesn't answer. Maybe it is too much to ask a new friend, but Erika agrees to pick her up, and only a short time later, they're sitting together in Erika's car.

"I mean I knew we were signing away some of our rights when we went under but this...I didn't think of this," Erika says, tapping her steering wheel as they idle in Ita's driveway.

"Who co-signed your consent forms when you agreed to treatment?" Ita asks her.

"My parents, who I appointed as my medical power of attorney. I don't think they understood why I was doing this. They still don't understand how much the pain affects me, though my mom is diabetic and has her own health issues. But we tried everything else."

Ita nods, feeling that connection deeply.

"When I went under, I was beyond caring. I didn't want to live, so I didn't really care what they did with my body. But this is so much worse than I thought. I should have known they wouldn't let me die or take care of me for free," Ita says. It's the first time she has spoken these thoughts aloud. Erika squeezes her shoulder.

"Thank you for telling me."

"So, are you in?"

Erika's hand drops to her lap. "Do you think we can do it safely on our own?"

"I spent all night reading as much as I could and I think we can. Clearly they don't want us to. Makes me want to do it even more."

Erika hesitates a moment longer, then starts the car. They drive to the clinic. Erika waits in the car while Ita tightens her mask and goes into the clinic under the guise of dropping off the signed packet. At the front desk, she slides the packet in the sealed envelope across the counter to the secretary and asks to use the restroom. She waits until the nurse, who is prepping the psilocybin liquid for someone's port, goes to get another pair of gloves before pocketing four vials.

She and Erika are already driving off when Ita imagines the secretary using her manicured nails to open the envelope and pull out the packet to file. The woman will see that VOID is scrawled across Dean's signature in Ita's handwriting, and on Ita's signature line, "NO FUCKING WAY!"

In the state park Ita chose, which is an hour outside of town, Ita and Erika traipse into the towering trees until they find a soft spot where the grass is thick and cool to lie down. They pop the metal seals off two vials and each drink one down. Holding hands, they stare up at the wispy clouds, the treetops, the cerulean sky. Ita remembers, in her worst moments, daydreaming about her death and how she would donate her body to a body farm, or compost herself in some way. She used to imagine her body in a mossy forest where decay took over its natural cycle and mushrooms fruited from her melting skin, making a home in her corpse.

"Try to picture somewhere we can both exist. Let's make a new dream."

Beneath them things are growing. In their minds, synapses fire, adapting new pathways, not ones where pain is nonexistent, but where it is shared, where their bodies feel more deeply than ever before through the contact of their skin as they hold hands. Ita pictures the rainbow hammock hanging in her parent's backyard, and soon Erika is with her, lying by her side, except the hammock hangs between the peaks of mountains under a boundless sky.

SICK WOMEN HOLD ON

USERNAME: @CHRONICALLYCUTE365
Some days I feel like I'm screaming
into an endless void.
I appreciate this community so
much,
but when things get really bad, I
feel like I'm beyond help.

USERNAME: @FIBROWARRIOR358
Hang in there friend. Please know
that you are loved and we need you
to stick around

USERNAME: @CHRONICALLYCUTE365
Sometimes it feels like I'm already
gone

She cleaned up the vomit from the toilet seat and bathroom tiles. Old and fresh sweat soaked into the fibers of her yellowing cotton sheets, deep into the bedrock of the mattress. The salt of tears long dried swept the corners of each room in the house, her first house, her first sanctuary.

But that was the problem. She wasn't alone.

The part of her that must have died that night, falling asleep next to the toilet, cried from the mirror above the sink.

The part born from her restless nights in deep, frothing pain thrashed against the other side of the bed.

The part that couldn't leave the house even if she'd wanted to stared out the window, and can only be seen in the dappled sunlight across the floor.

The sick woman wondered, what tied her other selves here? Besides the money sunk into renting this home she could no longer afford, she had sunk herself, her own DNA into the house. For a sick person, sometimes the place where they can scream and cry in unabashed wilting is the only place where they can be free.

Her mother intervened after the last late-night phone call when she'd moaned across the line, wondering aloud in a haze if she should drive herself to the hospital. Her mother insisted that her daughter break her lease and move back in with her parents so that she could get the care that she needed, at least for now.

"You won't be able to afford the house if you can't work. These episodes are getting worse and worse. Let someone else take care of you, please." So the sick woman who was only getting sicker acquiesced and allowed her mother to come in and box up her things, some for her old room and some for storage. But at night, when her mother went home, the sick woman walked across the warped hardwood floors and touched the windows, the mirror in the bathroom, the other side of her mattress, everywhere she could see and hear and feel her other selves trapped in their agony loop.

When she moved back home, she knew she would have to put that mask back on for her parents, if only to ease the creases around her mother's eyes, if only to make her father stop saying, "I wish I could take this pain away from you and into my body." Didn't he know that was impossible? He would crumble to nothing within the hour. Only a body conditioned by pain could keep burning and breathing and living in its rhythmic hold.

She wanted to comfort the screaming figure on the other pillow. She was like a lover mussing the sheets, but would not stop writhing, even when the sick woman ran her hand rhythmically along her arm like she did to her own self to calm the nerves. The self in the mirror could be muffled with the sick woman's hand over her mouth, but her wet screams left a heady condensation on the sick woman's living palm that made her stomach roll. The one who stood at the window shimmered and shook but left only dust on the woman's fingers. The truth was, she liked looking out the window too. She loved drinking her morning tea on the porch with her cat Gizmo before work, reading poetry and watching the neighborhood wake up. She wondered if her other selves remembered doing those things.

It wasn't so much that she missed them, but she couldn't bear to leave them here for the next renter to ignore.

USERNAME: @CHRONICALLYCUTE365
Hi All. Just wanted to let you know
I'm doing ok.
Family is taking care of me right
now. But I feel very attached
to my home. I've really loved
having this place to myself and

```
know I will miss it when I move
out. Any advice for how say
goodbye?
                    DIRECT MESSAGE: @FIBROWARRIOR358
            Some people like to cleanse their
            spaces
            when they leave a place. I can
            send you
                            some instructions.
```

The night before she was supposed to leave, the sick woman laid out a book on shadow work on the red and orange braided rug in the living room, the last remaining thing in the room since her parents had packed away all her furniture in storage. She lit a tall black candle and spread out some items on either side of it items she connected with in hard times: her lavender oil, a worn powder blue hand towel frayed from use as a cold compress, the heating pad she used almost every day, a book of poetry she'd been reading for over a year from a poet she both admired and felt insulted by, a poet who was more in touch with their body than she was.

The sick woman read down the page of the book on shadow work that described the ritual she was performing: "Thank these objects for their service in your life and how they have held you together." And she did thank them, running her fingertips along the items, so familiar and wondrous. They would go into her backpack tomorrow on the drive to her parents' house. She read aloud into the flickering quiet of the room,

"Shadows are not bad, they are simply parts of ourselves that we ignore, that we don't always want to face. Maybe they are parts of ourselves we need to let go of, or parts of ourselves that we need to forgive so that they are no longer holding us back from our truest forms. Begin by breathing deeply and imagining these shadows. Meditate on their forms, where they

come from, and confess them out loud. Only through the act of honest confession, free of shame, can we begin to heal."

She closed her eyes and hummed, low, deep in the back of her throat in a place she didn't recognize but trusted. She visualized her dead selves, her shadow selves, a trinity of pain she knew but could not recognize once outside of her body. There was shame there, yes, to see her pain projected in front of her and unable to do anything to stop its feedback loop. Is that what her parents felt when they tried their best to care for her? That was agony itself.

The sick woman kept humming, shaking her shorn black hair into her eyes, cut the week before with kitchen scissors in a fit of destructive want. There was something to this meditation, this humming, she was getting somewhere as she rhythmically moved her hands up and down her outstretched legs till her hands burned from the friction of her skin against the fabric of her pajamas.

When she opened her eyes, there they were, her three selves swaying in the shadow of the candlelight. One cried and coughed, the other looked forlornly at the body it once inhabited, the other reached out their hand. The sick woman stood up in front of them and, in an act of confession, addressed each one.

"I'm sorry," she told the first one, who stopped retching violently and blinked at her.

"I don't hate you," she told the middle one, who stood straight and nodded.

"I forgive you," she told the third one whose cold hand she took in hers and squeezed.

The three selves took hands, their bodies burning bright in a flash that collapsed together like a storm sucked into a wormhole. In their absence, a glistening clear stone fell to the floor. It was milky, smooth on one side and on the other side were jagged spires.

In the morning the black candle was burned down to a puddle of wax that dripped a trail to her bare feet. She had fallen asleep next to the stone, which her cat was trying to push with his fat gray paw.

"It's too heavy for you," she told him, scooping the stone into her backpack as she heard her mother's knock at the door. When her mother reached for her backpack so the woman could put the cat in the kennel, her mother complained, "What do you have in here, rocks?" The sick woman smiled at her feet. She would let her mother carry it for now.

USERNAME: @CHRONICALLYCUTE365
Me and Gizmo are officially
moved out.
I'm sad, but hopeful that things
will get
better. It's hard to accept when
you need
help, but here I am.

USERNAME: @FIBROWARRIOR358
You're right, it is hard. Sometimes
it feels impossible. But care is
something we deserve,
not something we should beg for.
Sometimes that
starts with turning that inward to
ourselves.

BUT WHAT IF YOUR BABY GROWS UP TO BE A WEREWOLF?

Jules leaned back in the padded sea-green chair each time the door to the clinic opened, letting out the AC, letting in the late August heat and the voices of a few sign-carrying "protesters" circling the parking lot. Thankfully, having Ryan there to flank her made a difference in how virulent their abuse was.

Her hands felt stripped of dexterity, floppy and loose when she held the pen and tried to finish filling out the intake paperwork with her medical history. They'd driven seven hours to get here, stopping for gas in Midland, where Jules had downed a ginger ale for the nausea. Now she really needed to pee but knew they were going to ask her to wait to take a pregnancy test even though she'd already had three blaring positives in her purse. It was procedure. They had to be sure before they could prescribe her the medications she needed and be on her way.

When the nurse called her back, Ryan asked if he should wait in the waiting room until she was done. "This is our decision, not just mine.

You should be there too," she told him, and so he lumbered behind her, squishing himself into the chair by the exam table while Jules stripped off her clothes and he held out his wide hands to bundle them together, folding her panties into her jeans like folding dough over in a bowl. Jules put on the starched medical gown, only bothering to tie the strings together at the neck. Who cared if the doctor saw her ass when they came in? They were going to see a lot more anyway.

They waited, and waited, Jules swinging her legs rhythmically from the exam table, and just when Ryan got out his phone to show her a funny pug video to take her mind off things, the doctor knocked and came into the room. A nurse followed her wheeling the ultrasound machine.

"Hi Julia, I'm Dr. Silva. It's nice to meet you," the doctor said, flipping her sleek black ponytail over her shoulder to shake Jules's hand. "Is this your partner?"

"Yes, this is my boyfriend, Ryan." Ryan leaned forward and engulfed Dr. Silva's hand in his.

"It's good you have him here to support you. So you said that you took some home pregnancy tests that were positive. What made you think that you are pregnant?"

Jules thought back to her last cycle over three months ago, to the ripping, screaming pain, the blood she had grown accustomed to seeing flow from her body. How awful that the absence of this rending change was her first sign something was wrong.

"I haven't had my period for three months. My breasts are tender and my stomach feels bloated and I've been having a lot of nausea."

Dr. Silva nodded along as she sat on the rolling stool and scooted closer to Jules, who had her hands crossed on her lap. The doctor pulled on sterile gloves and Jules almost laughed to see Ryan's horror as the nurse smoothed lubricant on the vaginal wand to prepare it for the doctor. As if Jules had never been violated in her life.

"Thank you for sharing that. That certainly sounds like some early symptoms we usually see during pregnancy, and of course the pregnancy tests seem conclusive too, but just to be sure, we're going to do a vaginal ultrasound. After that, we can discuss some treatment options. Does that sound okay?"

Dr. Silva's voice had a comforting tenor, like a hand smoothing down the side of her face. No wonder her clinic came recommended when she'd searched it out through a secure Discord channel helping people access reproductive healthcare out of state.

"Yes, that's fine," Jules murmured.

"Okay, I'm going to have you lie back on the table and scoot down until your bottom is on the edge of the table and you can put your feet in the stirrups. Let me know if you feel uncomfortable at any point."

Jules scooted down, feeling like the sterile paper on the exam table was going to rip underneath her. She glanced at Ryan, and he looked down at his shoes. It must be hard, she thought as her butt leaned on the edge of the exam table, to see your partner be poked and prodded like this. She was sure he'd never witnessed someone getting a pelvic exam or an ultrasound before this.

"Ok, I am going to insert the wand now. You will feel some pressure, but I am going to try not to cause you too much pain, okay?" Jules nodded, feeling the unwelcome intrusion of the wand inside her, pushing one direction, then the next. She took in the whooshing sound of her uterus from the ultrasound machine but the screen was turned away from her toward Dr. Silva and Marie, the nurse.

"Okay, we are in. Your ovaries and uterus look healthy," Dr. Silva told her, maneuvering the wand back and forth inside Jules as though she was trying to access a hidden passage in the dark.

"Okay, now I am seeing an embryonic sack here that has some pretty clear definition. And...yes there is a fetus here. Measuring almost twelve weeks actually. You said it was how long since your last menstrual cycle?"

Jules's breathing slowed. She closed her eyes, counted again in her head, then opened them again to find Dr. Silva, Marie and Ryan staring at her. She let out a lungful of hot air.

"It's been about three months since my last cycle. We had," she said and glanced at Ryan, "we had sex right around then."

"Hmmm," Dr. Silva hummed while Marie pressed buttons to take pictures of the fetus. "Okay, removing the wand now. Some pressure and then you should be good." The heavy instrument slipped out of Jules and she immediately arranged the medical gown to partially cover what had just been open and visible to everyone in the room.

"We're going to step out and let you change. There are some sanitary wipes in the drawer by the sink and some pads if you are spotting. Then I'll be back into in a couple of minutes to discuss your options."

As soon as the door closed Jules hopped off the table and waddled over to get some wipes to clean the lubricant from her thighs before she got dressed again. Her legs were a little shaky so Ryan held her panties and pants out for her to step back into. He rubbed his hands rhythmically against the soft fur of her arms. This at least was aftercare they both knew how to give each other. After each transformation, they would both awake in different rooms of the house, their clothes scattered, covered in viscera, lying among the animal carcasses they hunted in the wide woods around the commune property. Often, one of them would awaken first, stretching away the residual pain, and seek out warm damp cloths and robes so they could clean each other and recuperate together.

Jules wanted to believe this was an extension of that care, but this time it was happening to her body alone, not his; she didn't know how to help him traverse that gap in his experience. In fact, she didn't know if she had it in her to even try.

There was only so much they could do to prepare for their monthly transformations, but there were rituals. The whole commune had individual spaces where they could transform, some even preferring to be chained up to prevent them hurting themselves or others like a bad horror movie, but others took advantage of the enclosed outdoor spaces with reinforced fencing; they preferred to change as a pack. Ava, one of the elders, always emphasized to new folks that it was their choice and that everyone deserved privacy or help to cope.

Ryan normally chose to change alone. He was already so big, and in werewolf form, he would grow to ten feet tall, his claws like knives, and a long brown snout with canines that could tear through skin in seconds. When Jules transformed, she was smaller but no less terrifying, lean and sharp as a spear. Ryan preferred a secluded area in the woods of the compound, and Jules normally changed in her designated room where she could thrash and rage, and eat the poor panicked chicken caged in the corner in relative peace.

She didn't know why that night, that moon cycle, she chose to pursue Ryan to the red oak tree in the woods of the compound, the one with his long claw marks like deep wounds in the bark. It was the full wolf moon of January; something thrummed in her blood, and before she completed her own transformation, she wanted to see Ryan change in his element, away from everyone else. It felt intimate in a way, to share this between them. Jules waited in the bushes for Ryan to come stalking over. He slipped off his t-shirt and jeans, already soaked with sweat, then his boxers down those hairy, powerful brown thighs, and finally his gray wool socks, folding them neatly into a wicker basket by a bush. They would be collected later for washing and mending.

Ryan stood still, head tilted up to the vibrant moonglow, breathing slow and steady while his hands opened and closed. He remained still for so long Jules wondered if something was wrong when she heard a grunt of unmistakable pain. Ryan leaned forward, thrashing like he was covered in acid burning through his skin. Black lines ran along his arms and legs, up his muscular ass and broad back, and soon the skin began to rip along seams where blood welled up immediately, followed by thick black hair, the same color as his long hair he normally wore back in a ponytail but now hung loose over his face. The rippling, ripping of his skin was helped along by his long claws as the bones in his hands broke one by one, elongating into points. Ryan used his claws to rip away the rest of the human skin on his arms and legs, panting all the while. The skin that fell from his body hit the ground and melted into bloody pulp that seeped into the ground. Jules had never heard his werewolf voice.

She was feeling the bubbling of transformation under her own skin, the dark lines running along her veins, but while she was still conscious in this state, she wanted to see this part of Ryan. If Ava found out, she would rail at her later for taking this risk. Even mated pairs who had never met in this form could tear each other to pieces in panic, and she wasn't even in her final form yet.

The night opened its mouth, letting out the howls, close and distant, of her pack in the commune. Her friend Alex might be close by. He loved to run the woods as much as anyone.

Ryan stood at his full werewolf height now, huffing in the moonlight. He looked magnificent. That was the only word that echoed in Jules's mind before she fell forward, clutching the tree in front of her as the transformation pulled her under its dark waves, like drowning in the warmest gentle sea. Her teeth morphed from well worn to sharp and new and a bushy brown tail sprouted from the base of her spine. She was on all fours.

*Warm, warm, **so** warm all over*
       ***cold wolf** moon*
     ***here, he** is here with wolf*
    smells birds** mice rabbits smells all around **us
       his smell here
   *he is **wolf** with wolf clutching claws around **wolf***
  me wolf
want more *all his warm hair against wolf back*
claws in the dirt *blood in the dirt skin in the **dirt***
    ***wolf hold** wolf hold close closer take wolf*
 *from **behind***
   *he is **wolf** mate*
     ***mate** with this wolf body*
powerful thrusting *again again again*
    ***make** him part of me*
       part of this wolf night

Dr. Silva sent Jules and Ryan off with the prescription for mifepristone and misoprostol to complete the abortion in the relative comfort of the Days Inn they were staying in. They picked up more ginger ale and a large pepperoni pizza and a sausage pizza to hunker down for the night. Once Jules inserted the pills in the bathroom and put on the extra-large pads, more like diapers, that the clinic gave her, she put a towel down on the bed with Ryan while they watched Law and Order re-runs, the flickering glow of the TV lulling her into stasis.

In the hotel room, Ryan held her close as he had when they awoke that morning after, covered in their own blood and fresh, raw human skin. Tonight, her body cramped and flexed, but no blood came. Her body refused to let go.

"You should have come to me as soon as you knew," Ava growled at them when they returned to the compound the next day. She pushed her long graying frizz from her eyes. Their wolfish matriarch, their clan's protector. Her canine teeth remained too big for her small mouth, and when she smiled, or grimaced, her wolf showed too.

"I'm sorry. We didn't know what to do," Jules mumbled. She hadn't lived at home since she was fifteen, but the instinct to look chastised in front of a maternal figure still lived in her. Ryan looked down at his shoes too as his big frame crowded their small communal kitchen.

"And you don't want to keep it?" Ava asked. Her question didn't hold judgement, still it made Jules wince.

"I didn't even know that was an option."

"There are always options," Ava said, pouring hot water from a kettle over tea bags in three mugs and sliding two across the counter toward them. "I'm not going to lie and say I know what will happen if you decide to have a cub. But it will be a wolf, there's no doubt in my mind."

"I don't want that," Ryan said behind his cup. Jules looked up at him, studying his expression. "It's not out of shame. I can handle who I am. Who we are. But I don't feel comfortable making that decision for a baby who will always have to hide who they are from the world. We were already grown when we were turned. It's too much," he said, then looked sheepishly at Jules, adding, "at least for me."

"James was born wolf. Wish he were still around, we could have asked him more about his experience," Ava said.

"James wasn't the most well-adjusted person either," Jules reminded her, taking a sip of her tea. "His pack members weren't exactly the nurturing type."

Ava nodded vaguely, holding her mug but not drinking.

"I don't want to have the baby either. Not just because I don't want this life for them, but for me too. It's only since joining y'all the last couple years I feel like I have a handle on who I am. How could I do that pregnant? I'm not saying never, but I am saying not this, not now."

One thing Jules always appreciated about Ava was that she didn't treat her like her feelings or opinions didn't matter just because she was nineteen. They all knew the control their wolf-selves had over their lives.

"That's why you couldn't end the pregnancy before—this isn't something a few pills can fix. Then the best way to take care of this is to induce your cycle naturally. You mated in wolf form, now you need to take care of this in wolf form too, at least as far as I know."

"I haven't transformed since it started. How do I induce it?"

"Stop taking your monthly dose of wolfsbane. We'll have to sequester you more than normal, maybe even chain you up, but that should end the pregnancy. And in the future, you'll take better care," Ava warned.

Jules swallowed down the bitter cold of her tea and nodded. Ryan took her hand.

The week of the full flower moon loomed heavy on Jules's body. Everyone else in their pack began drinking their tea, including Ryan, the week before, collected and dried by Janis, Ava's partner. While everyone took their doses of tea together in the kitchen, Jules chose to wander the woods, her skin feeling dry and tight against her bones, the urge to scratch and claw at herself almost unbearable. It felt like electric currents were running across her muscles and nerves, and it took a lot of back rubs from Ryan to keep her from tearing into herself.

It hadn't felt like this since her first wolf cycle right after she was changed at fifteen. She had never known pain like that night, and Regaen, her maker, was no comfort. He was in his twenties, a loner adrift after high school, and at the time she found him so exhilarating to be around, even when his mood turned from charming to sour, even when he yelled at her unprovoked. When she snuck out at night to fool around with him in the woods behind the gas station down the street from her house, he told her he had a secret he couldn't trust with anyone else but her. She'd felt so honored, so proud to be with this handsome, thoughtful man, until he changed. Regaen chased her through the unfamiliar woods, biting her neck and shoulder so badly she had the thin white scars to this day. She went to a clinic without her mom knowing, claiming she was attacked by a stray dog, not really understanding what was happening to her body until Regaen showed up before the next full moon to drag her into the woods again. He told her he was thrilled to help her become someone new, better than she was before.

That first time, her very cells felt as though they were bursting open within her. Her nerves were aflame, from her hairline to her toenails, as everything ripped open across her body to let the wolf out beneath her skin. In the distance of her mind, she remembered Regaen laughing in wild delight at what he had done to her. In the morning, Jules woke up naked and alone, smeared with dirt and her own blood. Jules wished she could go back now to her teenage self and wrap her in blanket, help her home and tell her that every-thing was going to be alright, that her body was still her own. But that would have been a lie she couldn't even tell herself now.

Ryan was taking a stronger dose of wolfsbane tea than normal, as Ava and Janis advised so he could remain with Jules during the transformation. "You gotta stay sober, so to speak. Be her designated werewolf," Janis chuckled in her husky smoker's voice. When the pain settled into Jules's bones, they moved her to a reinforced shed on the property where she and Ryan would lock themselves in for the duration of the cycle. The shed still felt like outside since the floor was woodland dirt, but the walls were wood and steel.

"Are you ready?" Ryan asked her, helping her out of her clothes and setting them aside.

"Not really. But here we are." Jules hugged her arms around herself and sat cross legged on the damp earth floor. Ryan also disrobed and sat across from her. Though she'd seen his naked body many times, it felt absurd, and endearing, to watch him pull his long muscular legs into such an ordinary, peaceful pose. He held out his hands and she laid hers on top, letting him enclose them in his. It had taken her so long to grow accustomed to this sort of tenderness from her partner, to even believe she deserved this care.

"Tell me when you start feeling it, and I'll let you go, if you want me to," he said.

"Don't let me go."

Jules felt her heartbeat grow deep and erratic in her chest. The rippling of lightning pain roared through her limbs, the change unleashed. She must have been hurting Ryan, gripping his hands with her claws as her fingernails fell off. Her human teeth fell from her mouth, cascading down around them like the glass beads she used to use to make jewelry as a kid, making room for fangs so sharp they cut her tongue. Her fur erupted from her skin. She broke away from Ryan as her ankles stretched to long hind legs, the howl moaning out of her wolf mouth.

wolf is not alone with moon tonight

mate is with wolf

hurt hurt hurt like never before hurt

> *wolf claws the dirt*

> *hurt too much   cramping rolling hurt hurt hurt*

blood is coming now

> *blood gushes onto wolf's hairy thighs*

more blood than wolf has ever smelled

> *Mate laps up all the blood before it sinks into wet earth*

licks the blood from wolf's legs

> *wolf can curl up with mate until blood is gone*

In the morning, Ava would fry Jules up a ridiculously huge, rare steak in the cast iron skillet, saying "You need the iron," and hand her a large mug, the biggest they had, of turmeric and ginger tea.

Ryan would wrap her quilt around her shoulders and they would sit on the porch in the early morning light, birdsong echoing in the tall pines around them.

They would rest their weary bodies, maybe even cry in relief tinged with bitter reality, tending to each other as they always had, in only the ways they knew best.

THE BODY IS A HORROR CLASSIC: AN ESSAY

Finding the culprit

In John Carpenter's 1982 sci-fi horror classic, *The Thing*, a group of American researchers are attacked by an alien life form that can imitate other life forms and transform into them, feeding off of their bodies. When the alien is mid-transformation, it takes on a hybrid body made up of all of the life forms that it has consumed to survive.

In one pivotal scene, Kurt Russell's character, MacReady, tests the blood of each of his teammates to see which of them might be the alien in disguise. He heats a metal wire with a flamethrower because the creature reacts to heat and then presses it into a petri dish filled with each person's blood. His team members wait with bated breath as their blood sizzles against the hot wire, until one teammate's turn comes and his blood explodes out of the petri dish in a violent reaction to being exposed as the real monster.

I love this scene for how it depicts both what is hidden in the body and what can so easily be revealed. If only there were such a simple blood test to confirm so many maladies of the nerves, the muscles, the brain and the unspoken things that live inside.

The alien, the "Thing," is the antagonist, the monster in the horror film, but what is most terrifying about this film is how easily this alien creature invades and takes over the bodies of others to the point that they do not know that they are becoming a hybrid thing capable of swallowing their teammates whole. It is a film about how the alien sows discord and distrust among the team to the point of violence, but it is also a film about how easily we can lose the ability to trust our own bodies.

This has been my life for six years, navigating a neurological headache condition that gradually progressed to a debilitating point where I need daily preventative medication and ongoing care to be able to function from day to day. Even with imaging and diagnosis, doctors I work with cannot give me an answer about why I have daily pain and migraine episodes that can last for days. Was there an injury to my brain stem or is there a blood vessel pressing against my trigeminal nerve that sets off the pain? Was the nerve damaged by a virus? Or, is this neuropathic pain, where my brain has forgotten how to not be in pain and my neural pathways only know how to send false alarms? I cannot pinpoint the moment where my body was overtaken by this unknown force, I can only care for it like the beautiful monster that it is.

There is no shortage of films, television, comics, and horror media that depict the real and imagined horrors of inhabiting a body. Some of them are exploitative and often miss the point of body horror entirely, which is to show that what we fear the most is that our bodies will age, change, decay and die without our consent. This is not supernatural at all but a reality. What makes these stories successful is not how much they make people cringe or want to shut their eyes, but how they make people understand that we are all vulnerable, something that people who live with chronic illness and disabilities know all too well.

We know that there are often not clear-cut blood tests, radiological imaging and solutions that lead directly to a straightforward diagnosis and treatment. Sometimes diagnoses can take years, if they ever come at all, and a body in pain, a sick body without a solution, is exhausting to healthy bodies. Nothing has made this more clear than living through the Coronavirus pandemic with no end in sight. Countless apocalyptic horror films depict life after a virus has swept the world and killed millions, but not how governments and societies abandon those most vulnerable to fend for themselves. The kind of discord sown by not knowing who is vaccinated, who will be wearing a mask, who takes your safety as a vulnerable person seriously, is one small horror story after another that happens every single day.

Sinkholes

Carmen Maria Machado is a master of creating stories that show how patriarchy, trauma, and violence can transform a woman's body. In her graphic novel, *The Low Low Woods*, women of the town "Shudder to Think" are continuously transforming into hybrid creatures in response to the violence and forced amnesia visited on them by the men of the town who would seek to harm and control them.

One of the characters transforms into a deer-person, another teen girl becomes a living sinkhole, her trauma an inherited pain from her mother as her body opens a hole to the earth.

When I trace the origins of my sinkholes in some of my old journals in an attempt to learn where everything started, when my headaches began, I find an entry that charts my second year of my graduate program, the peak of my physical and mental exhaustion in a program that was called "community" but felt like a place where my energy was being swallowed whole. On the page, I have noted an assault, a violation by a man in an authoritative role. The next semester, I remember clearly trying to drive the hour to campus from my home to meet a professor I was assisting and having to pull over into the parking lot of a motel to vomit over the side of my car door from the pain throbbing in my left temple. In the six years since that first headache that stopped me in my tracks, I had always looked to the pain as a problem in my body to solve and not a place where chronic stress, exhaustion, and the subtle violences of academia unlocked the dormant pain in me.

In the book, Vee and El are two best friends who are on a mission to discover what happened to them on a night that they can't remember and how to help the other women in the town who have been violated by the men there. They are able to find a mushroom that causes the forgetting to begin with and one that makes a person remember their trauma. In the end, they leave it up to the women they encounter to choose to remember, or to live in the forgetting.

The elixir of remembering is to document, to resist forgetting, and to make peace with the one and only body I have.

Point of no return

Sometimes pain is a quiet invitation, starting behind the eye and slowly spreading out to the other regions of my face. Sometimes it is a scream through the body. Sometimes sleep is the only place where pain cannot follow me.

Other pains come and go. The prick of a needle to start an IV, sore ankles from wearing the wrong shoes, cramps and indigestion, but this pain is the only pain I can recognize like the voice of a growing storm as it rides in underneath my skin and makes a home in my body.

I have lain in bed during a headache so intense I wanted to scream, to scratch out my own eyes, to do anything for relief. When the pain comes, the last place I want to be is in my body. Pain can strip away the limitations of shame to the point where my insecurities about the sweat collecting in the rolls of my tummy or my mussed, stale hair after being in bed for two days are wiped from my brain.

I have felt a magnitude of pain that crescendoed to a space where there was no pain, like I was transcending the feeling of pain, where I could experience something untouchable across portals, across time. I felt energy and life running through me like pure fuel, and if I didn't calm my body I would burst into flames and burn alive in my bed, in my house with me in it.

This kind of pain is not dissociation. There is no relief in these moments. There is only the higher consciousness that comes with understanding that pain has ripped you open and laid bare the most truthful, screaming you.

Bloody transformation

When werewolves transform in films, their bodies come undone. Sometimes this transformation happens beneath the skin; knuckles expanding, bones breaking and swelling, hair sprouting. Other times, the wolf inside the person bursts through their skin and they are made anew. In all these depictions and stories, the transformation is excruciating. But pain leads to power. The ability to defend oneself, and to inflict harm, to release what has been fighting to get out.

In some of my favorite monster shows and films like *Supernatural*, *Penny Dreadful* and even the very campy *Van Helsing*, transformation into the werewolf, the monster within, is both violent and inevitable.

These kinds of transformations are the closest I have come to seeing how the body is capable of tearing itself apart and surviving, the violence internal, a form of care.

When I miscarried, I couldn't look away from the blood gushing out of my body, over my underwear, even running down my leg and smearing across the bathroom floor, so much blood that my protective animal brain told me that I was dying, though my body was reacting exactly as it should to the four pills that I had inserted inside of me to begin the process of releasing the contents of my pregnancy, my not-yet-but-still-mine baby who the doctor told us was not growing, and had no "heartbeat," the fluttering electrical pulse of growing life.

The feeling of clumps of tissue slipping out from inside of me was what I wanted, to rid my body of a not-alive baby who was not yet a baby and never would be. At six in the morning, I felt the most intense cramp that sent me running to the bathroom just in time to feel the largest bit of tissue burn through me and plop into the toilet. Sweating, with tears in my eyes, I cleaned myself as best I could and looked down at the full blood moon floating in the toilet water. Why do I want to immediately call it a moon? Does calling it a moon make it sound more sacred, more tied to the natural ebbs and flows of what can happen to the body? After a time, when my heartbeat slowed and my clammy hands stopped shaking, I forced myself to flush the toilet, leaving behind no trace.

I envy the monsters in the monster movie for their transformation, their ability to be torn open and become something more than they are, their pain, their scar tissue healed instantaneously through the power of monster magic. They are not left with remnants and scar tissue that reminds us of how transformation and the creation of life can go horribly, horribly wrong.

The Madwoman stays home

Bodies, like houses, can be haunted. The houses are described like faces looking out onto the world, the windows are eyes staring out, the door an open, gaping mouth. In the Netflix adaptation of the *Haunting of Hill House*, the infamous Red Room is described at first as the heart of the house, and then as the stomach that digests the family and their pain, leaving nothing but broken spirits behind.

In other stories, there is only one person who haunts the house, the woman who has been locked inside, or who cannot leave, having nowhere else to go. She is mad, or disfigured, bed ridden, her torment a contagion that must be kept from the eyes of others.

But then a virus spreads, a pandemic ravages the globe, a country, and a community. In a time of social isolation, now she is not the only one.

Now, she is no longer the old crone, the sickbed wife, the unhinged woman in the attic, the witch who chases children from her front lawn covered in weeds. She is simply the woman in pain who stays inside to heal, to prevent more pain, and though the world rages and cries around her, there is something about being at home that allows her to retrace her steps, to remember the self that she once was, and remake the self she is now.

The world slows down, the world is grieving for the dead of now and the dead of the past and the living blood and bones of this world and so she sees that grief as remembering when no one else wants to. She sits in her hammock, she reads the beautiful words of others, she tries to write down some of her own and makes a sanctuary out of small loves at home.

Unearthing

Damage lingers. There is still so much that I am learning about what the body holds onto.

After my miscarriage, I had a D&C, the surgery to clear my uterus of the contents of my pregnancy, the one that would allow my uterus to become a blank slate. Without knowing it for two years, this procedure caused scar tissue to grow in the wake of the scraping of tissue. This reaction is called Asherman's Syndrome. The scar tissue had grown to the point of blocking my fallopian tubes, causing infertility.

A hysteroscopy with the possibility of more procedures to clear this scar tissue from my uterus was necessary to make this chronically ill body a home for another being where it can grow. As the doctor described the procedure to me in her sterile white exam room and how my case was more "severe," I pictured her sawing away at a coral reef, a colony of growth inside me. My body has healed in its own way, protecting me and impeding me at the same time.

After the surgery, I was shown pictures of the insides of my uterus. Thankfully, my case was less severe than the doctor had originally predicted. Still, I was shocked when I saw that one of the photos showed a small yellow flap of tissue, a piece of placenta that was still adhered to my uterine wall. It sat inside of me for two years, the reminder that our bodies hold onto grief in so many ways.

When I first started writing this essay, I was healing from my last hysteroscopy, a post-surgery balloon and catheter inserted into my uterus to keep scar tissue from forming. My loved ones asked me how I was doing, and I had no words then to describe the absurdity of getting up to go to the bathroom to allow the blood from my catheter to drain into the toilet, a "normal" part of my recovery.

Three miscarriages and five surgeries later, I am left struggling with how fertility makes you consider what you have to lose. Now that I have stopped trying to be pregnant, giving my body and heart time to heal, I must acknowledge that in a post-Roe world, being pregnant is literally a choice to risk my life. There is a deep hope to be able to get pregnant and to have a child safely one day. Yet in my bones I am terrified to bring a growing being into a body that is unstable. I am afraid of my own pain, yes, but I am more afraid of being a mother in pain.

Unfurling

Body horror speaks to our realities; these stories depict being infected, changed without consent, and the loss of control that so many of us feel. What if we told more stories about embracing the monster, the unruliness inside?

In her book, *Women and Other Monsters*, Jess Zimmerman writes about what we can learn from the monstrousness and ugliness of Medusa in Greek myth: "The freedom of ugliness includes the freedom to make a new kind of beauty, a kind that nobody's thought to denigrate or control—to create it out of your body or blood or out of the dirt or out of the stones of the people you petrify."

In another life, I am not thinner, or perfectly healthy; I do not even live without pain. In that life, doctors listen and help me to understand the best ways to care for me. I want nothing more than to embrace the grotesque and beautiful in my living body. I lean my ear close and listen to the whispers of my body through the cracks in the walls.

ACKNOWLEDGMENTS

Thank you to the following publications where these stories and pieces first appeared:

First, I must extend my gratitude to the Undertaker Press team for their care and enthusiasm for my weird little book.

To Diamond Braxton for editing and publishing my essay, "The Body is a Horror Classic" in *Defunkt Magazine*.

To Richard Z. Santos for choosing my story, "Detached," to be a part of the *Night of Screams: Latino Horror Stories* anthology from Arte Público Press.

To *Uncharted Magazine* for publishing "Open Wound."

To Stephanie Rabig for choosing my story, "Holding Space," to be part of the *Broken Olive Branches* horror anthology for Palestine.

Thank you to the Texas and greater horror community, including the folks I have connected with at Ghoulish Books and the Ghoulish Book Festival and the Horror Writers Association, including Max Booth III, Lori Michelle Booth, Miguel Villa, and Ryan Bradley.

Much gratitude to the wonderful writers and friends who gave me feedback and encouraged me to write more speculative work and horror including Liz Clausen, monica teresa ortiz, and many more.

To Ramiro, my love and partner who reads my work with an open heart despite knowing just how weird it can get.

A READING LIST OF SPECULATIVE WORK AND BODY HORROR

The following is a list of books and media that inspired my work in this book:

1. *Eat the Mouth That Feeds You* by Carribean Fragoza
2. *Her Body and Other Parties* by Carmen Maria Machado
3. *Fruiting Bodies* by Kathryn Harlan
4. *Fruiting Bodies* by Ashley Robin Franklin
5. *An Altar of Stories to Liminal Saints* by Rios de la Luz
6. *M is for Monster* by Talia Dutton
7. *We Are Here to Hurt Each Other* by Paula D. Ashe
8. *Sister, Maiden, Monster* by Lucy A. Snyder
9. *Montrilio* by Gerardo Samano Cordova
10. *Nightbitch* by Rachel Yoder
11. *Lakewood* by Megan Giddings
12. *Eartheater* by Dolores Reyes
13. *Bat Eater and Other Names for Cora Zeng* by Kylie Lee Baker
14. *Song for the Unraveling of the World* by Brian Evenson
15. *The Secret Life of Insects and Other Stories* by Bernardo Esquinca
16. *Mine: An Anthology of Body Autonomy Horror* edited by Roxie Vorhees and Nico Bell
17. *Bound in Flesh: An Anthology of Trans Body Horror* edited by Lor Gislason

WRITING ACTIVITY

Write a story about a bodily transformation that suddenly takes place for you or a character you have created. What was the catalyst for this transformation (illness, violence, pregnancy, possession, etc.)? How will the character meet this change?

ABOUT THE AUTHOR

Leticia Urieta (she/her/hers) is a Tejana writer from Austin, TX. She is a teaching artist in the greater Austin community and is also a freelance writer. She is a graduate of Agnes Scott College and holds an MFA in Fiction writing from Texas State University. Her work appears or is forthcoming in *Chicon Street Poets, Lumina, The Offing, Kweli Journal, Medium, Electric Lit* and others. Her chapbook, *The Monster* was published in 2018 from LibroMobile Press. Her hybrid collection, *Las Criaturas,* from FlowerSong Press was a finalist for the Sergio Troncoso Award for Best First Book of Fiction 2022 from the Texas Institute of Letters and a finalist for the 2024 Next Generation Indie Book Awards for Short Story Collections. Leticia's poetry chapbook, *Offerings to a Tumbled Temple,* was released in 2025 from Purple Ink Press.

www.leticiaaurieta.com

instagram.com/leticiaasu

tiktok.com/@leticiauauthor

bsky.app/profile/leticiaasu.bsky.social

If you are a fan of horror stories and tales, you'll want to follow Undertaker Books.

We're bringing you stories to take to your grave.